THE
SEA SPIRIT
FESTIVAL
THE CHRONICLES OF NEREZIA - 3

THE SEA SPIRIT FESTIVAL
Copyright © 2024 Claudie Arseneault.

Published by The Kraken Collective
krakencollectivebooks.com

Edited by Dove Cooper.
Cover by Eva I.
Character Portraits by Vanessa Isotton.
Interior Design by Claudie Arseneault.

claudiearseneault.com

ISBN: 978-1-7389259-4-0

THE CHRONICLES OF NEREZIA

AWAKENINGS

FLOODED SECRETS

THE SEA SPIRIT FESTIVAL

STORIES FROM THE DEEP
(Coming January 2025)

MOTES OF INSPIRATION
(Coming 2025)

RUINED HISTORY
(Coming 2025)

LOST TRADITIONS
(Coming 2026)

TANGLED PAST
(Coming 2026)

UNDYING LOYALTY
(Coming 2026)

THE SEA SPIRIT FESTIVAL

THE CHRONICLES OF NEREZIA - 3

Claudie Arseneault

Kraken
Collective

This book is written in Canadian English. If you are unfamiliar with it, it may appear to "switch" between American English and British English spellings. Those are not mistakes; the words are spelled as intended. Thank you!

NEREZIA

(LOWER CONTINENT)

Horace (e/em), Embo Extraordinaire

Excitable and talkative, Horace has taken half-formed skills from eir many failed apprenticeships to become the Wagon's main cook.

Aliyah (they/them), Mysterious Stranger

Left with the strange ability to transform into an eldritch tree and the memory of a mystical forest, the quiet and perceptive Aliyah is on a quest for answers.

Rumi (he/him), Anxious Artificer

Rumi travels the world in a magical Wagon and springs his marvelous creations on the isolated cities of Nerezia. He disguises protectiveness and anxiety under pessimism and grumpiness.

Keza Nesmit (she/her), Thorny Protector

Confident and abrasive, Keza is a thorny companion who knows her worth. Under the spikes hides fierce and loyal love.

So far in
The Chronicles of Nerezia

Horace's trial day as a guard for eir home city of Trenaze should have been simple: stand watch, guide locals to the correct stalls, and guard the giant glyph that maintains one of the city's protective dome—the only thing that keeps away Fragments, shards that haunt the world and possess people.

But when a mysterious figure in a porcelain mask deactivates the dome, Fragments rush into the market, fusing into a monstrous amalgam. They are saved by a strange elf who can transform into a tree-like being, and who dissipated the Fragments with a single, eerie sentence: your story is my story.

From the moment it is uttered, Horace knows the sentences holds true for em, too—and when the elf collapses in the middle of the market, e carries them to safety, to recover away from the panicked crowd and inevitable questions.

This stranger, Aliyah, has but one desire: to

leave Trenaze's safe boundaries and find the forest that haunts their dreams. After an afternoon of board games in their quiet, sharp-witted company, Horace is ready to follow. They leave with Rumi, an anxious artificer and travelling salesman, in his Wandering Wagon of Wondrous Wares, a semi-sentient self-propelling wagon which always remains safe from Fragments.

Life on the road is, for the most part, filled with quiet hours cooking and cleaning, playing board games with eir two companions, or listening to Aliyah's stories of magical worlds. But adventures inevitably find them.

The first, at the Dead Archives, a secure waypoint where Horace is once more assaulted by the porcelain-masked figure—an Archivist. They call Aliyah "the Hero", capable of awakening Fragments, and berate em for being too weak to protect them. Horace's skills are immediately tested when Fragments possess dead bodies and attack, and the Wagon's crew barely escapes with their lives.

The second, as they seek to cross the Tesrima Ridge, and the pass through the mountain range is flooded. They are joined by Keza, an abrasive felnexi who'd only just assaulted them for their food supplies.

The water is trickling down from overflowing waterways blocked by Fragments. Between a small bomb from Rumi and Aliyah's powers, they dissipate the Fragments and reestablish the waterways—but one of the shards hurt Rumi badly, forcing Keza to steal away with him to her secret village. Unfortunately, the *secret* part is inscribed into their laws, and when Horace follows, e puts Keza into even more trouble. E has a brief chance to meet her nine wonderful kittens before the verdict falls for her crimes: exile.

With nowhere to call home anymore, Keza joins the group on their journey as they cross the flooded pass and head towards the coastal city of Alleaze.

Our records show that Alleaze was once a series of tiny fishing villages sharing a protected bay. Their quaint refusal to unite into a single city and their existence out of the Empire's territory had made the bay a prized tourist location. How it evolved from there into the sprawling Spirit-revering port of today, little is known. Fragments arrived, and where so many towns died, they flourished. I cannot help but wonder what the Hero's passage will bring to it, and how they may grow from it.

Archivist Neomi

1
Downpour

Horace had forgotten what it meant to be dry.

Rain drenched eir hair, weighing eir curls down, and eir clothes clung mercilessly to eir back and legs. The training stick in eir hands had turned slick and slippery, and Keza knocked it out of eir grip with a sharp thwack of her staff. She looked as miserable as e felt, russet fur flat against her bony frame, her ears low and her tail slinking to the ground.

"That's enough for today," she said, the grump in her voice an echo of eir own moodiness.

When the first drops had fallen three weeks ago, Keza had insisted that they keep training no matter the weather, and Horace had hopped to it with enthusiasm. If e wanted to get better, e couldn't skip days for minor inconveniences, and the morning ritual with eir new friend and mentor helped ground eir routine.

Life had found a simple flow. E woke up, ate a quick and light bite, put dough to rise, and climbed onto the Wagon's roof to train. The exercise opened eir stomach, so e'd eventually return to prepare a heftier breakfast for the group. Keza would follow and perch herself on the beams across the Wagon's ceiling to nap while e cooked, aided by Aliyah, who over time had gone from watching in silence to becoming eir fruit and veggies chopper-in-chief. Rumi was always the last to crawl out of his bed, dragged out by the enthralling scent of a delicious meal.

The remainder of the day varied more. Rumi tended to vanish into his workshop to tinker while Keza disappeared outside once more, to forage for supplies that could be used for dinner. Aliyah and Horace played games or exchanged stories—Aliyah was an endless source of those, their dreams filled with flying ships and floating cities, magical crystals and extravagant outfits. Sometimes e cleaned the Wagon or repaired clothing, and in those periods, e'd catch Aliyah in their own training, staring at their fingers as they hardened and lengthened into branches. Horace tried eir best not to peek, or to be subtle doing so; when e had met Aliyah in eir home city of Trenaze, they'd transformed into a full, terrifying tree-being, but it had seemed involuntary and painful. A few weeks ago, they'd learned a little control, and now… Horace wanted to ask, but the one time e'd built eir courage to it, Keza had interrupted, dropping in from another foray into the forest, dripping from the endless rain.

"I hate this forest and I hate this rain. What is *wrong* with the sky, that it won't stop flooding?"

She flicked her tail hard, sending a spray of water against the curtains of Rumi's workshop. His head popped out, mischief shining in his lizard eyes. "Maybe it just doesn't like you. Never had any problem before you came aboard."

"Keep it up if you want to starve." She

plopped a basket full of gigantic mushrooms on the table to underscore her point. "I don't see you foraging."

"Busy tinkering, sorry," he said. "Creating wonders like my wonderful little fur drier. That offer's still open, should you desire."

Keza hissed at him. "You come within a meter of me with that machine, and I'll hang you out to sleep in the rain."

Horace couldn't tell whether Keza meant it or not. She probably did, but the playful aggressivity had become an integral part of her relationship with Rumi. E didn't understand it, but e was a fierce proponent of live and let live. Besides, the two of them could be entertaining to listen to, and distractions had been few and far between since the rain had started. As long as neither seemed too bothered…

"I believe our suffering is coming to an end," Aliyah said, interrupting the fight before it could begin.

"We don't know that," Keza said, throwing Aliyah a quizzical look.

"I do," Aliyah replied. "There is something in the air. It is…" They wavered, their brow furrowed. "I think I feel the Fragments stirring."

They had all learned not to question Aliyah's sensitivity to the Fragments, or their relationship to them. All of Horace's life, e'd considered Fragments mindless shards bathed in golden light that roamed the land, forever in search of someone to inhabit, a possession that ended with the host dying of dehydration or hunger. But since e'd met Aliyah, the Fragments had kept exhibiting strange behaviour: fusing into a larger entity, stealing corpses as bodies instead of living ones, ignoring people to stubbornly carry out a task… E didn't know what to think of it. Their best hypothesis was that Aliyah's very presence provoked the changes, that they awakened the Fragments.

Horace didn't like this idea, but it was supported by the Archivists—or one of them, anyway. A mysterious person in an orange cape and porcelain mask who had let the Fragments through Trenaze's shield dome and assaulted

Horace, battering em for being too weak to protect Aliyah—to protect *the Hero*, as they'd said. Well, Horace had found emself a mentor now, one who believed in em, and e had no intention of allowing anything to happen to Aliyah.

"Stirring?" e asked. "Were they quiet under the rain?"

E'd not seen them while training, but eir attention had been focused on Keza's teachings. Besides, Fragments avoided the Wagon, staying at a considerable distance from it. Horace doubted e'd have spotted them through the curtain of rain and gigantic trunks.

"Or I felt more unmoored from their presence. It is difficult to say."

Regardless of the source of the change in the weather, Aliyah had been right. They whiled away another evening with games under the steady drum of rain, but it was gone come morning. No tap-tap-tap on the Wagon's wooden ceiling, only the regular creak of its big wheels as they turned, trundling of their own accord along the road.

Horace rolled off the mattress and barely remembered to fling a shirt on before e clambered down from the loft, then up the ladder to the Wagon's roof. No time for routine today! Outside, a bright sun greeted em, so blinding it drew a surprised hiss. Keza, always up early and already on the platform, laughed as eir vision adjusted.

Horace's eyes first latched onto the Tesrima Ridge, where they'd come from, and which now seemed so distant. It peeked above the trees, crowned by clouds and a dark curtain. No doubt rain still fell on its rocky cliffs, turning its paths into slippery death traps. Horace remembered standing on the Wagon's top as it crawled along the narrow trail down the mountains, eir gaze sweeping the landscape, scrambling to encompass the marvel of lush forest that spread at their feet and the faraway sight of water, lost to the fog. The sun had shone bright on the canopy, giant trees rising to the sky. Endless green unlike anything e'd ever seen.

Now e stared at these monstrous trees from

below, their bark the colour of eir home desert, their trunks so large e'd need to link hands with several of emself to circle them—and e was tall, with long arms. The green canopy was far above, vibrant and majestic, and e gaped at it as the rest of the crew came to enjoy the sun and until the Wagon crawled to a stop.

"If you think that's cool," Rumi said, "you should turn around."

So Horace did. E spun slowly on eir heels and gasped as the world turned from orange and green to pale yellow and endless blue.

They had paused on a rocky outcropping at the edge of the forest, and the earth below stretched into plains and ended in a great crescent moon bay with sandy beaches and rising cliffs. Its two arms of land curled around the turquoise water as if to protect it from the wider sea. And the sea… It had been raining ceaselessly for days, yet Horace doubted the water falling from the sky equalled even a fraction of the depths before eir eyes. The sea glittered in the sun, stretching until its darker blue blended with the sky. Blue upon blue upon blue, threatening to swallow Horace forever.

E pulled eir gaze away from it, fighting a bout of vertigo as eir mind struggled to comprehend the vastness before em. Instead, eir eyes latched back on the bay and the sprawling buildings that marked a city.

"Alleaze, the jewel of the Almari Bay."

Rumi swept his arms out, and it'd have looked more grandiose had he been more than three feet tall. Alleaze needed no help, however. Its squat and white building seemed to absorb the sunlight, and the square roofs alternated between from dark teal and bright red colours, giving the city a cheerful, inviting aura. It had no protective dome, nothing that Horace could spot to keep the Fragments out, and it existed as one, large sprawling mess. Horace stared at it as if e could comprehend its organization, but with every house and street on the same flat ground, spreading out from the bay's waters, e had no clue where to begin. Everything about Alleaze felt strange and confusing, and Horace had never been so excited in eir life.

"So what's it like down there?" e asked.

Rumi laughed. "What's it like? Can you, perhaps, be a more precise?"

Before Horace could think of a proper question, Keza cut in, an edge to her voice. "Are they friendly?"

"Of course!" He waggled a finger at Keza. "Most of the world *loves* outsiders, unlike a certain little village. Without us, they'd get no news from faraway places, and no goods either."

"So they'll welcome us?" Horace asked. "Do they have celebrations for that?"

"There wasn't one when I passed through last time, but that was a few years ago. And yes, they'll welcome us. Alleaze is particularly friendly, if memory serves. So talkative it's hard to escape conversations and get any work done. You'll love them, Horace, and they'll love you."

E grinned. That sounded like so much fun! "How long until we get there?"

"I'd say two days?" Rumi answered. "It's not as close as it looks."

Horace pouted. "Can't you make the Wagon go faster?"

The Wagon lurched right as e finished eir question, as if it had hit a trunk or a big rock. Horace knew better. First, it had been immobile. Second, it'd turned rowdy to express disapproval before, and even though Horace couldn't feel its rough emotions the way Rumi and Aliyah did, e could interpret the sudden movement well enough.

"Fine, fine, we take it slow," e mumbled.

"Slow is good," Keza said. "We've barely gotten to enjoy this area." She hopped on the platform's railing and balanced there, staff in hand. "I'll be out hunting. See if I can catch us something a little different to eat now that the rain's gone."

Before any of them could protest, she leaped off and sprinted into the forest, vanishing between thick trunks and low foliage. If it had been anyone else, Horace would have worried for their safety. But Keza was not only skilled with a staff, she'd mastered a technique passed down by her ancestors and which kept Fragments at bay, pushing them outward. When they'd met, she'd been stalking the mountain roads alone. She could handle herself out there.

"Gone before I can even get you up to speed about what few local customs I do know about," Rumi commented—and Horace spun to him with such speed he burst out laughing. "Sit, sit."

Horace didn't. E wanted to watch the city until it'd gone out of sight, hidden behind the forest's giant trees once more. After a moment, Rumi continued.

"First, their language isn't quite the same as Trenaze's. They're very close, but they've drifted apart enough that you'll struggle with the accents and some specific words being different. Just be ready for it. I think your ears will get used to it? Especially with all the talking *you* will wanna do. Second, when I was last here, no one introduced themselves with pronouns, and someone was kind enough to give me the rundown, so I'm passing it along.

"The simplest way to explain is that they use

four different pronouns, associated with four ... global perceptions of genders, you could say. It's not well defined, though I suppose it is more so than Trenaze's whatever-floats-your-desires approach. Each of these four has a corresponding colour, along with a pronoun set, and you'll see people wear various pins of all sorts—animals, plants, geometric motifs and so on—to mark which to use. Masculine, green, he/him. Feminine, orange, she/her. Many or fluid, purple, they/them. None or undefined, teal, e/em."

"So I'm ... undefined? None?" That was a strange thought. Horace wasn't certain what it was supposed to mean. E'd not chosen eir pronouns to *mean* anything at all. E'd just ... liked the shape of the sounds.

Rumi only shrugged. "Look, masculine is an ill-defined concept for me too, so I get. It's just not how we conceive these things where I'm from. But I put the green pin on because I like he/him, and I'm fine letting them think what they want, as long as I recognize when they're talking to me. At least all of our pronouns are in the lot. I'm sure you've met plenty of people in Trenaze with sets that don't match these four."

Horace had, though these four were the most common in Trenaze, too. Perhaps that was like the language being close: a resemblance based on proximity.

"I do not mind the purple pin, if it is simpler," Aliyah said.

"You'll notice a lot of Alleazans have multicoloured markers, too. As far as I could tell, they have these general gender spaces but aren't too uptight about where the lines are, and how often you cross them." He made a vague gesture midair, then shrugged. "If you want to know more, you'd have to ask them. I just learned the colours to get by."

Horace could do that, too, though e wondered what people would see in em, thinking that eir own teal pin meant *none*, or *undefined*. E supposed the second wasn't too far from reality, at least where defining emself within their categories was concerned. E didn't feel undefined, though. E felt like… Horace. It was hard to go beyond that.

Once his explanation was done, Rumi returned to his workshop below, to "work on doodads he might be able to sell". Horace swept the forest of giant trees and the coastal bay with eir gaze once again, then breathed in deeply. Everything was different here, even the air, humid and filled with new scents. Trapped in the Wagon, e'd begun to miss the familiarity of Trenaze, but now that it was dry outside and their next destination waited within view, eir enthusiasm burgeoned anew.

Horace spent most of eir morning leaning on the Wagon's railing, either taking in the forest still dripping from the recent rain, or studying the distant roofs of Alleaze when the landscape opened up. While Rumi had returned to his workshop to tinker, Aliyah had remained with em, their tranquil silence a habitual companion by now. They were one of the rare people with whom Horace could sit without feeling the need to talk, as if their presence filled the air where e'd usually put the words that otherwise burned eir lungs. This time, however, Aliyah was the one to speak first.

"It had never occurred to me how different forests could feel."

Horace didn't quite know what they meant, so they contributed the best they could. "The trees are very big."

It drew a gentle smile from Aliyah. "Yes, and very little springs at their feet. I suspect it is all up there." They gestured at the lavish canopy. "But in the forest of my dreams, the trees have thinner trunks, brown and beige and white, and they lean against each other, sometimes holding a fallen comrade. Bushes, ferns, and smaller trees grow everywhere, hiding away the ground, and moss climbs over rocks and trunks alike. It is very compact, almost stifling. This is airy."

"Sounds like the Wagon would have a hard time."

"Hopefully not, but we shall see when we arrive."

Horace wondered how long it would take

them. It seemed forever ago that Rumi had unfurled his map of the world and traced their path, from Trenaze in the desert, up along the Tesrima Ridge and through the Inari Pass, and now westward, to Alleaze, where they could find passage across the ocean. To a whole other continent e'd only ever heard of from faraway travellers and books of legends—and to the forest of Aliyah's dreams.

"I can't wait," e said.

They fell back into silence, staying until the sun had climbed all the way to its zenith then partly down, and eir stomach reminded em that open-mouthed wonder could only feed eir mind, not eir body.

2

Sailors and Tokens

Horace hadn't grasped the scope of Alleaze until the Wagon rolled into the city, and the entire crew gathered on its top platform. E'd known it was big, of course, but nestled as it was around the bay, that bigness had felt contained. Now that buildings sprawled in every direction, their pale and boxy façades giving the impression of a long, continuous wall, eir view of the surroundings blocked by houses several floors high and towering over the Wagon, eir perception of Alleaze turned to that of a maze of streets. E craned eir neck, watching as residents crowded their balconies to look at them pass, pointing and whispering. E waved at them and received a few hesitant gestures in return.

Over the two days it had taken them to reach the city proper, Horace had battered Rumi with additional questions about Alleaze. He'd not known nearly enough for Horace's taste, and perhaps more importantly, had not known if anyone was in charge of greeting strangers and housing them, the way Clan Viella would be in Trenaze. The last time Rumi'd come, he'd rolled his Wagon into a big marketplace, kept it stationed there, and sold his goods from it without ever visiting the rest of the city.

"They loved the gadgets!" Rumi had said in an attempt to defend himself. "Declared over and over that it'd bless them during the next Festival or something."

"Or something?" Horace had repeated, aghast. "Rumi, didn't you ask?"

Rumi had only shrugged, utterly unaffected by the horror in Horace's face. The curiosity would have eaten em alive!

E hoped e'd have a chance to correct Rumi's grievous negligence. E wanted to ask the people *everything* about their city: what the walls had been constructed with and whether the reddish roof material came from the desert; how they kept Fragments away without big domes; how they'd chosen the colours for their gender pins, and were those braided motifs on people's breasts and hats also indications; what they ate in daily meals and what was considered a luxury. E wished they'd remain in Alleaze for a long time, so e'd have opportunity to investigate anything and everything that crossed eir mind, but Rumi said their stay would depend on when the next ship sailing across the ocean departed.

"Do we know if there's even a ship to take us?" Horace asked, hoping for a negative response.

"Yep," Rumi said. "See those?"

He pointed ahead along the road, so Horace scanned for anything unique. They did have tiny flags and colourful strings hanging across the street, going to and from balconies and water gutters.

"The flags?"

"No, beyond that! The very big masts?"

"Oh!"

Boats. They had been talking about boats, and sailing out at sea, which probably meant a big ship. And ships were supposed to have masts, weren't they? E kept forgetting about the water, because the idea of crossing an entire ocean—as if the infinite blue had an end to begin with—was mind-boggling. But e could see multiple wooden masts through the strings of flags and over the rooftops, three of which dwarfed all others. A very big ship indeed.

Hopefully they had just returned and wanted a long vacation on solid ground. E'd find out soon enough, if the Wagon's steadfast progress through the streets was any indication.

For now, Horace absorbed the sights and smells—the bright splashes of teal and red roofs over white and maize walls, the strange aftertaste of salt on eir tongue, and a smell that reminded em of the forest, only … rotting, e'd say. It was hard to explain. Everything had a slightly distinct quality here, which Rumi maintained was the difference between dust and humidity. Horace liked it this way. Different was good. E wanted new experiences, new cultures, new adventures; e wanted the homesickness to be worth it.

They turned a corner and the street opened up onto a seaside area. On one side, large colourful tents surrounded an open fire, and merchants tended to long tables of fish and seafood, nets and poles, and other miscellaneous objects e'd never seen—tiny wooden fishes and colourful feathers, among others. Across from them rose several warehouses, wide doors leading into beckoning shade. Beyond, flat wooden constructions advanced into the bay, with boats of all sizes tied to them. Docks, and a lot of them, too! They extended along the coast for almost the entire span of Alleaze, curving with the beach. Many were empty at the moment, and eir gaze sought the waters. E gaped—though, honestly, e wasn't sure e'd closed eir mouth once since entering the city.

Out there, dozens if not hundreds of tiny boats floated on the water, sails curled up. They peppered the entire bay, sleek darkness against the beautiful turquoise, bobbing up and down with the waves. Cliffs rose beyond, the crescent shape of the land closing part of the bay off to leave a far narrower opening.

Horace had heard of ships, and read about them. They were the stuff of legends, of inaccessible lands only travellers saw, of lifestyles entirely unlike Trenaze's. E'd expected to be wowed by them, true, but not by how *ordinary* they all felt. Just so many little wooden cups that somehow floated; the most normal thing in Alleaze, no doubt.

"It's beautiful," e whispered.

"Terrifying, you mean," Keza retorted. "This whole place is, friendly or not."

She stood firmly in the middle of the Wagon's roof, her clawed hands tight around her staff, her pupils so big the irises had almost vanished. Her tail flicked in erratic patterns. Was she scared? *Keza?*

"It can be both," Aliyah chipped in. "It is certainly a great deal of people, is it not, Keza?"

Keza hissed in answer, her pupils narrowing as she turned to Aliyah. She *was* scared, Horace belatedly realized. Her village was small and isolated, a self-contained community that had secreted itself from the world. Keza might have known about cities the way e knew about boats, but experiencing the real thing was very different.

"It's okay to be nervous," e said.

"I don't want to hear it!" She thumped her staff on the ground. "And don't you slip a word of this to shortscales."

To shortscales? Wasn't Rumi right there? Horace cast eir gaze about, looking for Rumi, only to find out he'd gone back inside. The Wagon stopped with a small, jerking motion, locating itself in a cleared gravelly area near the entrance of the docks. Rumi hopped off from it and started away.

"Rumi! Where are you going?" e called. Rumi paused at eir booming voice.

"Booking our passage!" He gestured to a massive vessel deeper into the water—the one with the bigger masts he'd shown Horace earlier. "That's an ocean carrier and we don't want her sailing without us aboard."

"I'm coming!"

Horace scrambled past Aliyah and Keza—and heard the former's breezy laughter on the way—and clambered down the ladder to join Rumi, who had thankfully waited for em. Small as he was, he could easily have lost himself in the crowd, and Horace would have had no idea where to look for him.

E almost lost him anyway. There was so much to see at the docks! A pair of fishers unloaded a giant net full of their recent catch into a metal basin, another sat half-covered by a sail as she repaired it. A munonoxi stomped their hooved feet as they argued with an elf, the quick flurry of words at the limits of Horace's understanding, as if e knew them but couldn't quite draw meaning from them. E kept stopping in eir tracks to stare, and soon Rumi held eir hand as they snaked their way towards a long wooden building with a hanging sign.

The near darkness when they stepped in disoriented Horace, and e squeezed Rumi's scaled hand harder until eir eyes adjusted. By then, eir friend was conversing in rapid fire with a dwarven official—or at least, Horace assumed she was an official by the little badge matching the sign outside, right above her orange pin.

"The ocean carrier? You're looking for Captain Jameela Tar." Horace needed great focus to follow what she was saying, every word more lilted and flightier than e was used to. "S'nother dwarf, three braids, painted lips and blond beard, probably on the westmost dock. But don't get your hopes up."

As far as Horace was concerned, warnings *were* a reason to get eir hopes up. E didn't want to leave so soon! But Rumi frowned, and out of sympathy for eir friend, Horace forced eir brow to furrow.

"I like my hopes the way they are," Rumi said. "Thank you."

He received a grunt in reply, and the official moved to someone else.

They found Jameela Tar sitting cross-legged on a crate, in a loose tunic with pants underneath and a two-coloured swirl as a pin: orange and purple. She was relaxing, a long pipe stuck between her teeth and her head thrown back against the wall of a warehouse. Their fingers played absent-mindedly with the braids of their near-blond beard, and smoke drifted between their black-painted lips. Horace could not help but feel they were about to interrupt a private moment. Before e could touch Rumi's shoulder to turn them around, however, Jameela cracked an eye open.

"Newcomers," they said.

"Indeed!"

Rumi's voice had gone a full pitch higher and brimmed with sudden enthusiasm. It reminded Horace of the day they'd met, when Rumi had tried to sell em his magical air-sucking horn of amazingness—energetic and confident in a way he rarely was in private.

"I am Rumi of the Wandering Wagon of Wondrous Wares, and this is my associate,

Horace ka-Zestra. We're looking to negotiate passage across the ocean?"

"You're out of luck, buddy."

Rumi would not be deterred so easily. "I assure you, I have plenty to offer for your ship and your crew. My talents—"

"It's not about you." Jameela pulled the pipe out of her mouth and tsked. "Newcomers. You've got no idea what's happening, do you?"

"I'd love to know!" Horace exclaimed.

Jameela laughed and rewarded Horace with a smile. "All right then. First thing you should always do if you're in our fine city is look to the sea." They slid down from their crate and walked closer to the waterfront. "You see the lights there? Big circles in the water. The instant one of them pops up? That's our signal to end a cycle, and look forward to the Sea Spirit Festival."

It took a moment for Horace to find what Jameela was pointing at. Two distinctly paler circles could be spotted in the bay, diffuse and partially hidden by the sun reflecting on the waves.

"Oh!" Horace turned to Rumi, grinning. "You heard, Rumi? We're just in time for the Festival! We get to see it!"

Not that Horace knew what that entailed. But e would soon, wouldn't e? This was so exciting! Rumi ignored em, his gaze latched onto the lights, his tail giving an annoyed twitch.

"There's no way we can convince you to miss the event?" Rumi asked.

"Miss it?" The constant amused lilt in Jameela's tone vanished. "Master Rumi, you do not know what you're asking for, so I will let this offence slide, but let me make one thing clear: the Sea Spirit guides our lives. It knows every fish swimming these waters, knows to nurture the coral and its inhabitants, knows how the wind blows and the sun shines. It knows the bay; it *is* the bay. Only the most degenerate Alleazan would eschew its guidance, provided only every decade or so. I advise you never suggest such a behaviour of me, or anyone you respect."

Rumi snapped his teeth in a quick exasperated clack. "All right, all right. I didn't mean to offend. How long till you get the guidance you're looking for?"

"Who knows? The Sea Spirit will tell us when the time comes. We receive guidance on the fifth light. We've been at two lights for a while now. Everyone's booths, games, and trades are ready for the Festival, so the speculation is that it'll turn soon. The third light can be long, too, and we all love a lengthy Festival. The fourth is just taking things down, sealing some last deals, and it's usually pretty fast."

"So in terms of, say, number of sunrises?" Rumi prompted, all cheerfulness vanished from his voice.

"Twenty? Thirty? Maybe a bit more, even. Then I'll get the guidance. But only after sixth light has come and gone will the festival end."

"So let's negotiate now, for then! I'd rest easier with our passage secured."

Jameela laughed, a resounding cackle that sent Horace's heart for a spin. It was sharp and bemused, soaked in the joy of strange encounters and thrilling surprises, and it made em think of

Jameela as a kindred spirit, another lover of adventures.

"I don't know if I'll still captain the *Pegasus* when all is said and done." She gestured at the massive ship in the bay. "Might not even be a sailor, if I've erred and displeased the Sea Spirit."

Might not even be a sailor.

Might not even be a sailor.

Horace stared at her, the words an arcane string in eir mind, their meaning unintelligible. How could Jameela quit being a sailor? "I-I don't understand," e said. "Aren't you a *Nes*? That is — a good sailor, a master at it? Why would you stop *being* that? What would your Clan say?"

"I don't know about this clan business, but if the Sea Spirit directs me elsewhere, who am I to defy it?"

Jameela stuck their pipe between their teeth and took a long draw from it. In the small silence, Horace scrambled to understand the implications of their words. Did Alleazans simply ... rebuild their entire lives every time the Sea Spirit Festival happened? Did they have no aspirations, no desire of self-improvement? How could one strive towards mastery of one's craft if one's clan could change on the whim of a spirit?

"You're making a face," Jameela said. "Trying to be polite?"

Guilt surged through Horace and e sputtered a half-apology, as if e'd been caught with impure thoughts. Had eir confusion been that apparent? E hoped it hadn't come across as judgmental. It all *felt* wrong to em, but that didn't mean it was.

"Where I am from, we …" E searched for the correct words to capture the breadth of Trenaze's culture, how everything tied back to your work. "Your family—your people—are those you share your occupation with. We choose a role that fits us best, a vocation that brings self-fulfillment, and dedicate our lives to it. The most skilled become *Nes*, that is, masters at our crafts."

The more Horace floundered to explain, the higher Jameela's brow raised. They took a long draft from the pipe again, and exhaled slowly.

"Don't know how you get a functioning society out of that. Wouldn't trust any of us common folks to know what's best for the bay, and without the bay, there is no Alleaze. I gotta be honest, it sounds terrifying, having to make that choice for yourself. And be stuck with it for your entire life?"

They clacked their tongue, and the pop of disgust echoed across the busy docks in a simple, definitive indictment of Trenaze's civil organization. Heat climbed to Horace's cheeks, surging with eir urge to defend eir home. But all e could think was how often e'd entered an apprenticeship only to fail at it, to be rejected by the Clans. Even eir current name—Horace ka-Zestra—was a lie in itself. E didn't belong in Clan Zestra, not after e'd betrayed their trust to leave the city with Aliyah, and the truth of eir inability to fit into Trenaze left em bereft, powerless to protest Jameela's criticism.

"Nothing's perfect, but it sure makes planning easier when your life's not reliant on the whims of the local spirit," Rumi chipped in. "I suppose we'll have to return once the Festival's over and see who's in charge?"

"Afraid so. You might as well enjoy the festivities while you're stuck in town." Jameela blew another cloud of smoke, and her expression slid into thoughtfulness. She set the pipe down, and looked between Rumi and Horace. The corner of her black-painted lips turned up in a crooked smile. "I'm sitting here, with my pipe and my hopes I'll witness those good skills you got to offer, and hear all the wild tales you could tell, and I can't help but think, hey, if they play festival games and eat festival food, they earn festival tokens, yes?"

Jameela turned to them, as if expecting an answer to what Horace had first taken to be a rhetorical question.

"Yes?" e said.

They snorted. "You've never seen a token in your life. Of course you've got no idea where this leads."

They dug into their pockets and withdrew a handful of blue objects, the size of a coin but in a material Horace didn't recognize—some sort of metal alloy, perhaps? Each had been engraved with an animal shape, of which almost all details had been lost safe for two wide wings. Horace's fingers hovered closer, but e didn't dare touch the tokens. Something about them felt old and sacred, as if they belonged to another era.

"Thing is, the Sea Spirit guides us to our general roles: farmers, sailors, civil servants, acolytes, and so on. But there is great variance within these spheres, and who gets what precise job, well, that's a dirty game of politics. And these tokens? You can use them two ways. You can weigh the Sea Spirit's guidance, expressing your own desires to it before it chooses. Or you can keep them for later. Unspent tokens are normally worth a lot in the ensuing negotiations over specific positions. Except you're outsiders. All the tokens would be good for is as currency during the festival. You follow?"

Horace nodded eagerly, even though e had lost track halfway through, too busy trying to match the general roles to Trenaze's clans in an attempt to better understand this strange seaside city. Thankfully, Rumi had continued paying attention.

"Let me guess," he said. "We give you any extra tokens we've gathered, and if you're still a sailor, you use them to secure your place as the *Pegasus'* captain and take us aboard."

"Precisely! You win, I win, we're all happy and we sail together stronger from one successful collaboration!"

"That sounds great!" Especially the part about attending the Festival. The rest, e left it up to Rumi.

"All agreed, then. I'll give you a few tokens to get started." Jameela extended a hand, her palm turned towards the ground and otherwise flat, fingers pressed together. An awkward moment passed before she explained the motion. "In Alleaze, you seal a deal by piling your hands in the middle and holding seven seconds, for the seven roles of the Sea Spirit."

"Oh, right," Rumi said, clearly remembering from his last visit. "Get lower, then."

Rumi stretched to his tiptoes and placed his

hand atop Jameela's before pushing down until the pile reached a more comfortable height. Horace bent forward and added eir own, much larger palm. They counted up to seven, and every second weighed heavier on Horace, an invisible force pressing down on em. When Jameela removed their hand, e started breathing again.

Jameela tallied some twenty-odd tokens, adding a few after Rumi's insistent "there's four of us, actually", then offered him the bag.

"Some advice, before you head off: don't tell others you'll be handing the tokens to me, and they'll more readily give you some. As far as I know, strangers normally keep out of the Festival—no role to negotiate—so no one should expect you to pass them along. Besides that, have fun. Play the games, eat the food, and meet the people. It's a lively time in Alleaze; of celebration, renewal, and consecration. Make the best of it and come back with even more tales to share!"

Horace had never heard anything so exciting in eir life—or, well, maybe in the last hour. Exciting things seemed to happen a lot, in this journey, and e had no doubt there'd be more in the future. Filled to the brim with enthusiasm, e slapped Rumi's back.

"Let's get back to the Wagon and tell everyone the excellent news!"

"We're *stuck here*?" Keza hissed, her voice holding an angry terror Horace had never heard before.

They had promptly updated Aliyah and Keza on the situation. While Aliyah had remained silent, the curious quirk of their brow and renewed glint in their eyes the only outward sign of interest, Keza had grown more agitated with every word out of Rumi's mouth, until he'd informed her of the estimated twenty to thirty days of waiting and she'd snapped.

"No one's forcing you to come," Rumi said, "but unless you want to spend all that time squirrelled away in the Wagon, you'll have to meet *some* new people."

A low, displeased rumble rolled out of her in response.

"Come on, Keza," Horace said. "It'll be fun! You never know when you can find new friends. Just like we met you on the road!"

"I robbed you," she reminded em, but the bite had gone out of her voice, sliding into an amused exasperation e'd grown familiar with. "Horace, when did I ever strike you as the type to enjoy meeting people?"

"You talked to us," e mumbled, before rallying to another tactic. "If you stay here, you'll miss out on the games and local cuisine. I won't be there to cook."

Keza snorted and her tail flicked, betraying her disapproval. "Can't believe you're trying to get me with food." Or that it was working, if Horace heard the pout in her voice correctly. She turned towards Aliyah. "What about you, quiet one? Eager to mingle with hundreds of strangers?"

"I am curious about this festival, yes, and its Sea Spirit."

"If it's any consolation," Rumi said, "I'd much

rather stay in the Wagon and tinker on a few projects for the ocean carrier, but we've got a deal to uphold, and I figure I might find clients to sell other bits and pieces to. We can hole up a few days to recoup from too many people if need be."

"There *will* be need," Keza assured him, "but I guess we might as well get a better idea of what we're up against. When the third light comes up…"

"We go to the Festival!" Horace cheered.

3

The Sea Spirit Festival

When Trenaze held festivities, it took over the Grand Market for a few days, providing a central location for all residents to gather.

Alleaze, it seemed, celebrated throughout the city as a whole.

Every street was covered in decorations—some with colourful bunting flags marked with symbols, others with flower garlands, or large nets that had been dangled between balconies, or even strings of fish bones and sea shells glued together and painted over. Alleazans would have stalls right outside their doors, selling food and jewelry and clothes, or they'd stroll through the crowds with the wares attached to their body, hanging from their shoulders and on a small table. Everywhere Horace turned, people traded with tokens, chattering and laughing.

Pockets of the city *had* been dedicated to specific endeavours, though. A large portion of the docks held a gigantic fish market, with fresh catches and large specimens marked as "blessed by the Sea Spirit" —which, locals told Horace, meant they'd never spoil, and had often been caught months or even years ago. Sellers would label their age on little seashells or wooden placards, and these racked up far more tokens than regular fish. Across from this market was one full of nets, fishing poles, cages, lures, and a wide variety of tools Horace had never seen in eir life. When Horace started stopping at every table to muddle through explanations, struggling with the accents in the ambient noise, Rumi grabbed eir hand and pulled em away.

"Satisfy your curiosity later. Jameela mentioned games, and those are where we can win more tokens."

Even though e knew they had up to an entire

month in the city, e pouted. What if e forgot to come back?

"I want to know, too," Aliyah said. "We can return together."

That was enough for Horace. Aliyah had a much better memory than em. It was so good, Horace sometimes thought they absorbed information and never let it go.

In time, they found an old public square transformed to hold a host of games. Their first clue of its location came from jolly music and loud bells, tailed by laughter and excited cheering. Then the crowd thickened, the steady stream turning into a slow morass of people. Keza slunk closer to em, always on eir heels, and e was careful not to push between groups where she couldn't follow.

Eir mindfulness disintegrated when they reached the square proper, and all the options extended before em. Horace towered over a great deal of the crowd, and e had no trouble sweeping eir gaze across the grounds, absorbing the countless opportunities offered to them: a cluster of grills and cooking apparatus from which drifted a delicious scent—to snack between games, e figured—a plethora of stalls with challenges of luck or address, two very big vats filled with water with an obscure purpose, and tables with individual games and trinkets that, at a distance, reminded em of Rumi's work.

Horace's mind was spinning with the possibilities, and e couldn't decide where to start when a powerful voice boomed across the fairgrounds, burying the noise of the crowd.

"Do *you* have what it takes to be the Storm Catcher? Come, come, gather here and test your strength!"

Horace had no idea what a storm catcher was, but e had a fair amount of muscles and even more curiosity. E stretched on eir tiptoes, scanning in the general direction of the voice until e spotted a black-furred munonoxi with bulging biceps and tiny, clearly shaved off horns. The pronoun pin—green for he/him—had been tied to the horns, in bold display.

"Only two tokens to try!" the munonoxi

called. "Come on now, don't be shy!"

"Rumi," Horace started.

Before Horace could ask, eir friend had slapped two of the tokens in eir hand. "You show this town, Horace."

Horace grinned and bounded in the right direction, the rest of eir group on eir trail. The munonoxi's eyes locked on em as soon as e emerged from the crowd, even though e'd been approaching from his back, and the horizontal pupils tracked eir movement. Horace would never cease to be amazed by the wide scope of munonoxi's sight. E didn't know how e'd ever process so much visual information!

"I think we have a contestant!" The munonoxi slammed a hoof to the ground, and the public cheered. "Come, come!"

He gestured at Horace, who pushed eir way through the last of the crowd, stopping a step out of the tight circle of onlookers. The munonoxi wore a robe made of thick, multicoloured braids that wrapped around his body, folding in ways Horace didn't quite follow. The red, yellow, and green colours seemed almost fluid as he scooped up a gigantic wooden hammer and held it high for all to see.

"For seventeen years, I, Adelar Hilstorm, interpreted the Sea Spirit's guidance for the good people of Alleaze. Although my time as an acolyte has, for now, drawn to an end, I am eager to continue this vocation. So here we are, at the heart of the Sea Spirit Festival, celebrating as we wait for the Sea Spirit to choose its next Storm Catcher. But who will be the chosen one—the hero who will sacrifice all to replenish the Sea Spirit's strength, so that it may guide and protect us in decades to come? How does the Sea Spirit even choose? Some say it is willpower that makes one a Storm Catcher, others argue for piety or wits. But I? I say it is raw strength, pure and simple!"

He swung the heavy hammer with remarkable ease, then threw it up in the air for a spin, and caught it on its way back down. Keza whistled in appreciation.

"I think he argues for what fills his pockets," Aliyah whispered.

With the munonoxi's attention on em, Horace had to hold eir laughter in. Hopefully eir smile would be mistaken for admiration. Which it also was! That was an impressive feat, and Horace was starting to wonder if e was cut out for the task. E didn't think e could spin the hammer quite like that—or more precisely, that e would catch it again if e tried.

"My big fella, if you believe your strength worthy of the Sea Spirit, step forth! All you have to do is strike this here gorgeous carving of a shell with all you've got, and should your might prove sufficient, a Storm Catcher will rise!"

"I thought I was the Storm Catcher?" Horace asked. "Or, er, potential?"

"No! I mean, yes! It's—It's a metaphor, and not. Look, just hit the thing."

He extended the hammer, and although his grin hadn't budged, he sounded annoyed. Horace chose not to remark on it. Perhaps e'd overstepped with the question? There was so much e didn't know about local etiquette, and as much as e wished to ask, e didn't want to offend!

Adelar Hilstorm had a show to give, and Horace a shell to hit, so e grabbed the hammer and stepped forward.

E didn't have a lot of experience with heavy weapons. Clan Zestra had first trained em with a sword and shield, and e'd left before they'd had time for anything else. Still, over the course of eir many apprenticeships, e'd had to move quite a fair share of crates and other unwieldy objects. E let eir body remember those efforts, the way the weight had shifted with eir position, how a slight change in balance could affect so much. As the memories returned, e swung the hammer midair, getting a sense of its heft.

The crowd had hushed, a bubble of near silence amidst the noisy entertainment, and suddenly the fun game felt far more important. As if eir status as a potential chosen one truly hinged on eir success, and it wasn't all show dressing. E turned and waved to eir public.

"I think I'm ready," e said, to break to silence.

They hooted and cheered, some calling out bets for and against em, and the tension in eir chest eased. Better a simple game, in eir opinion.

"So what *do* I win, if I make it? Tokens?" e asked.

"Indeed!" The munonoxi stepped back with a bow and gestured towards another clam shell, as large as the one Horace was meant to hit, but upside down. A pile of tokens waited inside. "We've had a number of failures so far, and there's nineteen tokens up for grabs."

"Right." Horace spread eir feet in front of the clam. It was connected to a second similar shell, which covered a mechanism of some sort. Horace wondered what was hidden under it, but e figured there was only one way to find out. E slowed eir breathing. In … and out. In … and out. E raised the hammer behind em. In … and *out*.

Horace swung the hammer overhead and down hard on the clam. It hit with a thunderous smack, and the other shell lifted up with a snap, freeing a strange apparatus of concentric circles. Those shot upward into a multi-tiered copper structure, stretching up and up and up, each new tier unfolding with a satisfying click. It flew past

Horace's head, but even as the crowd gasped, Adelar made a pensive, doubtful sound.

And indeed, its rapid rise slowed just as quickly, inching to a stop a good five feet higher than Horace. For an instant, the machine seemed suspended there, its tip not quite completely deployed … then it started back down, collapsing in on itself, each tier sliding into the previous one as it sank back into the ground. Horace stared at the clam as it fell, latching into place. E had been so close!

"How unfortunate," Adelar said. He pocketed one token, and placed the other in the bowl. "I suppose the next aspiring Storm Catcher will have more at stake."

Horace pouted, the hammer still loose in eir palm. E wanted to try again! Something must have been off with eir weight transfer, or eir breathing, or the precision of eir strike on the clam. E could do better, e know e could!

E spun towards eir group, apologies and pleas on eir lips, to find Rumi placing two tokens in Aliyah's hands. They stepped forward, thin body half buried under their massive cloak.

"I'd like to try," they declared.

This time the crowd's silence was complete. Aliyah had no muscles to speak of and a frailness about them that didn't bode well for a show of strength. No one believed they could do it. Adelar didn't seem overly bothered—if anything, this would be easy tokens for him.

"Of course, of course!" he exclaimed. "Anyone can try, after all. You never know in whom our Storm Catcher hides!"

Aliyah undid the clasp that held their cloak, handing it to Keza before they came forward and offered their two tokens to Adelar. As his hands clasped around them, they turned to Horace.

"You did well." They extended their hand.

Horace gave it a squeeze of encouragement. "You'll do wonderful too, I'm sure!"

"Horace," Aliyah said, amusement creeping into their voice. "I need the hammer."

"Oh! Of course you do. I'm sorry, I—"

"The handshake is appreciated, too," they said, gently cutting em off.

Horace used the opportunity to retreat back to the group, lining emself behind Rumi as if eir small friend could hide em. Aliyah wrapped both hands around the handle and lifted the hammer, obviously straining to get it off the ground.

"Did they tell you anything?" Horace inquired to the two others.

"Nope," Rumi said. "Just asked for our precious few tokens."

They must have had an idea. Of the four of them, Aliyah was the most level-headed. They wouldn't waste the tokens on a whim. Many continued to whisper in doubt as Aliyah wielded the hammer and dragged themself into position. Once they had both feet near the target clam, mimicking Horace's stance, they turned towards Adelar.

"Tell me again, how the Sea Spirit selects its chosen, and what makes one a worthy candidate."

"I—hum, strength, that is, muscles and—"

"Please," Aliyah interrupted, calm but firm. "I

need the dramatic version to focus. Give it your all. This is a time for stories and entertainment, is it not?"

Adelar closed his eyes and readjusted his sleeves, then hopped and slammed his hooves down in quick succession, twice. It felt like a ritual, the way Horace moved through the same exercises every morning as part of eir training, or how e blew on eir saira dice before throwing them. When Adelar's eyes reopened, rectangle slits settling on Aliyah, all signs of being flustered had vanished. He bowed, then cast his deep voice out.

"Here in the beautiful city of Alleaze, the sun shines upon cerulean waters, and glittering gems of light sparkle on our most wonderful of wonders, the Almari Bay. We are not the Bay's jewel; that honour goes to the life thriving within the water, from which we draw subsistence, and to which we owe safety and joy. The Bay sustains us and we, in return, sustain it."

His tone had turned into a gravely, almost sing-song affair, and he swept the air with his arms as he spoke, moving about the space to occupy it. Aliyah listened intently, eyes closed, fingers wrapped around the hammer's handle.

"The Sea Spirit, guardian of the Bay and the water beyond, guides our lives. Every cycle, it expands its energy—its very vitality—to safeguard all that lives from the water, and every cycle, as its might dwindles and it senses exhaustion, it signals for help. Thus begins the Sea Spirit Festival, through which we celebrate its hard work, receive its guidance once more, and learn who among us has been chosen as Storm Catcher, to save the Sea Spirit and renew our future."

Horace caught a glimpse of a pale green glow crackling along Aliyah's skin and froze, distracted from Adelar's voice by the sight of it. The light wrapped around Aliyah's wrist then sank into their skin, thickening it into dark bark. Slowly, ebbing and flowing with the story of Alleaze and its Storm Catcher, it climbed upward, nearly invisible in the bright sun. If Horace hadn't seen it repeatedly while Aliyah had practised, e'd have missed it.

"To be the Storm Catcher is an honour, the perfect capstone to a fulfilling life. Only they can brave the howling winds and churning water to restore the Sea Spirit to its full power, allowing it to protect us for another cycle. Some say it is piety that draws the Sea Spirit to their chosen one, others argue it is strength of character, or wits, or even stubbornness. But I say it is brute force! The tonus of your muscles, the understanding of your body, of your physical place within this realm."

As the tale continued and Aliyah's magic took root, their arms turned into long branches, small twigs and leaves burgeoning from their elbows. The crowd's whispers intensified—many had noticed, now. Horace tore eir gaze away from Aliyah to study onlooker faces, but none seemed aggressive.

Then e spotted a porcelain mask, briefly visible between two older elves, and a flash of orange cape sent eir heart leaping into eir throat. An Archivist, here? They'd already vanished, gone as fast as they'd appeared, but e couldn't help eir cold sweat. The first time e'd seen an Archivist, they'd opened a hole in Trenaze's protective dome.

"It is time, challenger," Adelar declared, calling eir attention back. "Prove your worth. Smash—"

Aliyah obeyed before he could finish. They swung the hammer in one fluid strike, the bark from their twig-like fingers crawling over its handle, holding it tight. It landed on the clam with a resounding *smack*, interrupting Adelar and sending Aliyah bouncing up an inch from the impact—enough for Horace to glimpse small roots through their boots, tying them to the earth beneath.

The clam lid lifted, and the copper circles sprung upward, clicking in rapid succession as they rose towards the sky and stretched through every single one of the layers. The last settled in with a deeper pitch, then all was silent. When Horace tore eir gaze away from it, the bark had rescinded from Aliyah's skin. They held the hammer tight, and Horace would have sworn they leaned on it. Transformation always seemed to take its toll on them.

"Am I worthy?" they asked, the slight lilt in their usual serious tone the only indication of amusement.

The crowd answered with a loud cheer. Horace scanned it again, but couldn't spot the Archivist anywhere in it. Meanwhile, Adelar bowed with a sweeping gesture.

"I am impressed, O Storm Catcher. Please, claim your reward!"

Aliyah exchanged the hammer for a small pouch of tokens, and Horace hurried by their side, gripping their shoulder to help support them as e chatted happily about their performance. They trudged back to Keza and Rumi, who whistled and cheered.

"That was magical!" Rumi exclaimed before dropping his voice. "Like, literally. Was that wise? How did you do that?"

"It is hard to explain. His story had power," Aliyah said, before pressing their lips together.

They remained silent for a few seconds as a munonoxi detached from the crowd, eager to make an attempt of her own, then added, "Once I felt it, I had to try—to know if I could."

"Well," Keza said, "we're off to a great start! At this rate, we won't need to endure the hordes for too long."

Horace couldn't find any masks or orange capes in the crowd. E hadn't imagined it, though, e was certain of it. Maybe if e squinted harder…

"Horace?" Aliyah asked. All three were staring at em now, eir distraction noticed.

"I … think I saw an Archivist. Watching. They're gone now."

That put an immediate damper on their mood, and they all looked around except for Keza, who tilted her head to the side.

"Archivist?" she asked.

"Let's find another game," Rumi said. "We can catch you up, and keep our eyes peeled. I'd love a chance to give these assholes a chat."

The festival grounds had plenty to offer in the ways of distraction, and no Archivist reappeared as they moved from one game to another. Keza trounced everyone at a challenge of speed and agility where they had to throw wooden fish and sea food in the appropriate buckets, while Rumi unravelled "the puzzle of fates", a cubic contraption with various symbols on its sides, which could be rotated a dozen different ways and made Horace's head hurt. In time, though, Rumi had lined up all the symbols together, to the poor booth holder's great dismay.

The cheers and laughter of the crowd followed them about, punctuated by bells ringing and the deep, regular echo of a gong. Keza dragged them away from the thick crowd once, climbing to the roof of a random building to flop down there and let the wind calm her. Horace's own head buzzed from the constant effort of unravelling the local accent, but unlike eir three companions, who looked relieved by the pause, e couldn't wait to throw emself back into the thick of the crowd.

They eventually ran into a table where five contestants sat lined up, a symbol displayed in front of each, which Horace recognized from the puzzle game Rumi had solved: wheat, harpoon, scroll, spiral, chalice, and net. One seat remained empty, in front of the spiral—a whirlpool, perhaps?—and when the scent of delicious seafood and warm dough drafted to eir nose, Horace knew that was destiny. E scrambled forward, asking if e could take the last spot for the eating contest, and plopped emself down without pausing for the rest of eir team's protests. E could see them on Rumi's face and the angry flick of his tail. Keza didn't seem too convinced about eir chances either, but that didn't stop the excited swish of *her* tail.

"This seems like a horrible idea and I can't wait to watch," she said.

"E'll be sick," Rumi grumbled. "Don't count on me to clean the Wagon."

"I promise I won't be sick!"

Beautiful pies arrived just as e finished talking, still warm but no longer steamy. An

enormous pile was set next to em, as high as all the other contestants'. Most of eir rivals shared eir bulk, but one of them — the scroll contender — was a slender halfling. Horace wondered where they could even shove all this food. The pile was higher than them!

A judge blew a whistle and Horace dropped the mystery to grab eir first pie. E'd participated in a similar contest once, though they had been eating cactus fruits instead. E still remembered the juice trickling down eir throat with every bite and the intense sweetness of it all — a very different experience from the salty, potato-and-seafood stuffed pies. The mashed inside proved sticky, fighting every swallow, and Horace emptied eir water more often than e'd expected as e devoured a first pie, then another, and on and on. E lost track fast — of the pie count, of the cheering crowd, of anything but the weighty food in eir body, slotting itself in every corner of eir stomach, filling em until it felt like each breath was a battle.

A glance at the table revealed that all but three

participants had held on. The halfling was finishing a pie, licking their fingers as they gestured for another. The third, a muscular elf with hair so long it trailed to her lower back even tied and wrapped up, put down her pie as Horace looked.

"I-I can't," she mumbled, and even that sounded painful.

Only two of them, then.

When Horace returned eir gaze to the pies left for em, eir whole body convulsed. E picked one up. Maybe all e needed was to eat this one pie, to hold on just a little longer, and the halfling would give in. Just the one.

E took a first bite, and eir stomach heaved. A warning.

The halfling kept eating, shoving small bits of pie in their mouth at incredible speed, vanishing it all in their tiny body.

Horace put the whole pie in, and when eir body fought em, e slapped a hand in front of eir lips and swallowed down. Distantly, e heard Rumi call eir name. Eir gaze went up, but before it found Rumi, it latched on a bright orange patch.

The Archivist was back, standing casually among the onlookers, their head tilted to the side. This wasn't the same person Horace had met before. Their porcelain mask was different, featuring a smirk and a splatter of golden glitter, but more importantly, their shorts gave way to munonoxi legs, with thick thighs and a deep, almost purplish fur.

Horace jumped to eir feet to call out, and eir whole body heaved with the movement. E smacked both palms on the table, fighting the urge to return the pie into the world, and when e glanced back up, the Archivist had vanished. Farther down the table, the halfling was still cheerfully stuffing pie in.

"Honoured Stranger?" the judge asked, looking at em.

Horace sat back down and lifted eir hands in defeat, swallowing the rest of eir last pie. "I'm done. Wouldn't want to break my promise."

The judge whistled again, calling the competition to an end.

"Our winner this cycle is the incomparable Ludarin 'Crumbs' Fielding!"

The halfling hopped onto the table with a victorious whoop, then engulfed a whole other pie just to prove their point. The crowd roared, clamouring for another, and they obliged it. It made Horace feel better about eir decision. No way e'd have won that!

Second place still netted em a fair number of coins, so Horace didn't return empty-handed to eir team. Getting up and walking those few steps turned out to be a challenge of its own. E had never felt so bloated, as if pie threatened to ooze out of eir skin. Keza poked eir belly as a way of greeting em, and e was almost sick right there and then—and it would have served her right. She laughed at eir sudden face.

"Sorry, won't do it again." She raised two hands, palm open and outward, then added, "Training's gonna be a trip tomorrow, huh?"

Oh no. Surely e would feel better tomorrow?

Sure, it was already late in the day, and e had eaten enough for a month, but e'd sleep it off. Tomorrow would be fine.

4

Sink or Swim

Tomorrow was not fine.

Horace had barely slept. Eir entire body had chosen to revolt over the number of pies consumed, and e'd stayed sweaty and slightly nauseous all night. For the first time in months, e'd abandoned the shared bed with Aliyah and stretched out on the Wagon's roof platform, staring at the stars above. The evening was warm and humid, unlike anything e'd experienced in the desert. Even the stars felt changed, though Horace suspected e might be imagining that. The pink film of Trenaze's domes had always tinted the skies, and e probably couldn't tell the difference.

Adding to the physical uneasiness, e couldn't take eir mind off the Archivist in the crowd. Did every city have one? Were they tracking the Wagon and Aliyah? What did they want? How many of them were there? E'd told the others, but no one had answers, and until they did anything, Rumi insisted they keep going to the Festival and gathering tokens. Horace agreed, though e wished e could stop looking over eir shoulders while they played.

Then training came, and Keza did not spare em despite the lack of sleep and overabundance of food. In the end, however, the exercise helped em work through the worst of eir malaise, and by the time she'd finished pummelling em with her staff, e felt less like a stuffed plush bursting at the seams and more like a very bruised human. E limited breakfast to a couple of dried fruits, drank a lot of water, and they were all ready to go for another day.

Through their time in the festival grounds, they kept passing these two big tanks of water, above which two slim platforms had been installed. Two participants would stand there, each with three blunted javelins in hand. The goal was to throw the weapons at a beam under your adversary's platform with enough force to knock it out, cause it to collapse, and dunk the poor soul in water. The winner would reap what tokens had been bet by the two contestants.

The group had stopped there often to watch strangers play, but every time Horace had suggested that they try it out, Rumi had pointed out they'd be taking coin from one another, which would make it kind of pointless.

"It'd be fun," Horace had said.

"Don't sweat it, Horace," Keza had replied. "It's 'cause he knows none of you could beat me at that game."

Rumi huffed but didn't argue. It seemed he had taken it personally, because five days after that first discussion, when they passed the tanks again, he squared himself in front of Keza and pointed at her nose.

"I challenge you to the dunk tanks," he declared.

Keza laughed and stretched up and back, in a slow, lazy movement, savouring the long pose as he awaited her response. "Sure, shortscales."

When their turn came, they made their "pointless" bets, and climbed into position. Aliyah and Horace stationed themselves halfway between the two. No one in the crowd — or rather, no orange cape. Horace had only seen the Archivist once since the pie-eating contest, and that worried em as much as a constant presence.

On the two platforms, Keza hopped from one foot to another, her claws tapping against the wood. Rumi was, instead, completely frozen, one hand over his arm, even the twitch of his tail stilled by anticipation.

"Ready?" the booth manager asked.

"You bet," Keza replied, while Rumi nodded.

"Then start!" She slammed one of the blunted javelins on a flat metal instrument, and its bong echoed across the grounds, a now-familiar sound that had marked their time in the festival.

Keza grabbed the closest javelin and slung it.

It flew, clipping the pole under Rumi's platform and sliding it without knocking it out. In the split second she'd needed to do so, Rumi had rolled up his sleeve and lifted his arm. A simple machine was strapped over his dark blue scales, with an elegant tube the size of his forearm. He slapped a button on top, and two balls shot from the tube with a hiss of air and a pop. They spun, attached to one thick rope by the middle, and wrapped themselves around the support to Keza's platform, pulling it straight out from under it.

The rickety wooden platform collapsed, bringing Keza down with it. She yelped as the wood gave way under her feet and flailed all the way to the water below. It was by far the least elegant Horace had ever seen her, and e could not help the hearty laugh that escaped em as Keza thrashed in the water. Her feet found the bottom, she pushed herself to the surface, and scrambled out of the tank, fur clinging to her body and making her seem almost skeletal.

"Rumi, you cheat!"

Rumi leaned past the platform's edge, sharp-toothed grin on full display. "Who said I *had* to use the javelin?"

She growled and half leaped, half ran up the wall, her claws scraping against the glass until she landed on the lid of the tank, and kicked the support out of its remaining axis. Rumi was cackling long before his platform fell, and the skittering sound only cut when he hit the water right below. He swam to the edge, where Keza waited, flicking droplets with each of her tail's twitch.

"Well worth it," he said.

She shoved him back into the water.

Horace's ribs hurt from laughing long after they'd left the tank and returned to the Wagon, Keza promising retribution every step of the way and Rumi dismissing the threats as "water off his scales."

Although they paid for food and drinks with tokens, too, their pile had grown considerably over time. People seemed keen on offering them up even when they failed to win games, or simply refused to take compensation for a meal. Horace had thought Alleazans were all very, very generous people until Aliyah had pointed out they negotiated teeth and nails with other citizens.

"They would rather we have it than rivals," they'd concluded.

Ever since, Horace had hoped none of them had Jameela as a rival. It felt unfair, to take the coins without warning them where most would go. Almost a lie, and e had never been one for lies. But Rumi had forbidden em from bringing it up on purpose, reminding Horace that this was, in essence, how they paid for passage aboard the *Pegasus*.

As days passed, Alleazans became less generous with the tokens, however. Many of the festival stalls had closed down, now out of prizes, and the tension in the city seemed to grow with every new sunset. They spent less and less time at the Festival itself, and one morning as e was eating eir pre-training snack, Keza dropped from the rafters and startled em.

"I'm not training you today. You're training me."

"Mwht?" e'd asked, mouth still full. What did she think e could teach her?

Keza leaned in and lowered her voice. "You can swim, yeah? I'm not stepping on a floating pile of planks if I can't keep my head above water. So you're coaching me."

She *had* sunk pretty hard in the tank, after Rumi had dunked her. E'd thought it was surprise! Horace afforded emself the few seconds necessary to recover and swallowed eir thick slice of mango. The idea that graceful, athletic Keza couldn't swim baffled em, but e'd be happy to help if e could. Which was questionable. E *had* spent countless hours in the Underlake, inside and under eir home's mountain, but that water was very still. It didn't have waves, or currents, or whatever else the depths of the ocean might contain. That didn't mean e wouldn't try!

Beaming, e said, "Sure!"

Two hours later, they'd walked out of town to

find a deserted beach closer to the arm of rocky cliff extending into the sea, protecting the Bay. The sun twinkled across the deep blue waves, the wind caressed their skin without bringing about dangerous crests, and Horace couldn't stop grinning. They'd stripped down to their underpants, and e'd waded into the water, dove into it, and swam around until e could get used to the rhythm of the waves. Once e was more confident, e'd returned closer to the beach, standing in the water until it reached eir thighs. Keza had remained at its edge, each wave lapping her clawed feet. Every inch of her fur stood on its end, fluffing her up in a way that felt more adorable than intimidating, and Horace struggled not to laugh.

"I can't teach you if you don't get in the water first," e said, and the amusement e'd tried so hard to hide seeped into every word.

"I hear your chuckles," she snapped. "This isn't *funny*."

It was. Glyphs smite em, but it was. On solid ground, Keza was pure agility, climbing and perching and dodging and running as if nothing could tie her to the earth. She'd lorded it over em more than once in their training, and watching her stand by the water, puffed up and too prideful to follow em in shallow depths despite being the one to *demand* e taught her ... it was absolutely funny. Saying so wouldn't help any, however, so instead Horace raised one hand, palm out.

"I promise that whatever happens here will never reach anyone's ears."

"Especially not Rumi's," Keza added.

"Especially not Rumi's," e confirmed, eir grin widening as e imagined how much fun their little friend would get out of this.

Water splashed eir face, startling em. Keza had leaped into the shallows and swiped at the waves' surface, sending it flying at em.

E laughed "That's one way to start," e said, and retaliated with a splash of eir own.

Keza tried to dodge, but the density of water around her legs slowed her movement, throwing her off balance. She hissed, pupils widening as she fell and sank below the waves. She flailed about, and Horace was at her side in an instant, grabbing her arm when it next broke the surface. Her claws dug into eir skin as she pulled herself up, bringing her head above water. Keza heaved, her panic dimming with each pant, her fur sticking to every bony ridge underneath.

"I hate water," she spat.

"It clearly loves you," Horace chirped, laughter still singing in eir voice. Keza's eyes narrowed into slits, so e hurriedly added, "By the time you love it back, you'll move through it with the same grace you have on soil, and nowhere will be safe for us."

That earned em a vicious grin, and Keza shook herself, sending droplets flying everywhere and puffing out her upper body fur again. She spun her shoulders, stretched, then spread her feet on the sea floor; a routine e'd seen countless times when they set to train.

"All right, Big Hunk. Show me how to love the water, or whatever."

Her determination was tested as soon as they

started, when every attempt at floating on the water, limbs extended, had her sink within seconds. She always reemerged cursing and spouting water, and soon she was arguing with Horace about the point of floating without moving.

"It's learning how your body interacts with the world around," e retorted—words she'd used on em when e'd protested at long exercises of balance. Keza recognized her own comments instantly, and after a sputter and a little profanity, she returned to the exercise without further complaints.

It took a few attempts with Horace's hand under her back before she managed to float on her own. Wonder widened her eyes as she held the position, waves lapping at her sensitive ears, caressing her arms and legs but never running her over. She stared at the sky, not daring to close her eyes, until Horace leaned over.

"Ready to learn the strokes?"

They stayed almost an hour in the water, and while e wouldn't call Keza a competent swimmer after that, she no longer watched the Bay like an unpredictable enemy and could paddle with enough skill to keep her head above the surface. Horace hoped they'd get a windy day to practise churning swells—for eir own sake, in addition to Keza's. E worried eir experience in the still Underlake wouldn't help against strong waves and troubled waters.

They returned the following day, and the day after, spending more and more time in the water as the fourth light turned on, signalling for the end of booths and games, and a period to take down stalls and finish the last trades.

People begun gathering by the waterfront in "watch parties" with soft drinks and fresh fruits, to spy on the four lights. The docks were soon thick with Alleazans every night, but rooftops and waterside parks also drew their share of citizens. Horace naturally invited emself to one such reunion, eager to understand it.

E joined a stranger sitting on her own, tall and thin with a lengthy undercut and four rings pierced into her long, elven ear, plopping down on the beautiful sandstone bench, next to her. She turned, eyebrows raised in a silent question—e'd found, through eir stay in Alleaze, that they expected whoever made an approach not to waste time in greetings. It was hard, still, to skip the cheerful hello e so adored.

"I'm a bit lost." E spoke every word slowly. E'd gotten better at deciphering the Alleazan accent and learned a lot of specific vocabulary, but locals often asked em to repeat if e wasn't careful. None of them had the intense practice e'd had. "Why is the festival quiet at night? Why is everyone here?"

She stared at em while she unravelled eir words, and a smile blossomed as understanding reached her. "We wait for the Sea Spirit to tell us it has chosen our fates and is ready to guide us. It must be close; it rarely takes more than twenty days between the third and fifth lights."

Jameela had given the same timeline. It was hard to believe they'd already spent a solid twenty days in Alleaze. They had been a blur of games and interesting conversations, and e wished e had twice that amount still ahead of em. But from the sound of it, they would soon move on to the next step.

"And after the fifth light?"

"We go, one by one, to the bottom of the Bay."

"You swim to the bottom?" Horace exclaimed, and she laughed.

"No need to swim. It's an underwater shrine, by the northern end of the city. If you're ever on the other side of the docks at night, look. You should see its lights."

They talked most of the evening. She was named Valetta and yearned for a less manual role, so she could come home with more energy to help the elders she lived with. They discussed how many tokens she had to weigh her balance with, and Horace added a few—e couldn't help it, and Jameela wouldn't know if they didn't ask!—and wished her luck.

Except Horace also offered tokens to a hopeful soul the following day, and then the one after, until e decided to stop bringing tokens to give with em, before Rumi found out and scolded em. The conversations were enough to nourish em.

When Horace had first heard of this fate-assigning spirit, e had been horrified. Vocation was everything in Trenaze. It was who you *were*, and for years Horace had had no idea who e was supposed to be, because e couldn't find a Clan e belonged to. At home, e'd not even been a full adult yet, though e'd long outgrown the age at which others transitioned from Clan Nissa to their chosen family. The Forever Apprentice, they'd nicknamed em, and only when Horace had met Aliyah had e experienced a strong sense of calling, of belonging.

The people e spoke with in Alleaze felt neither immature nor bland and adrift in their sense of self. They knew what they aspired to, cared for loved ones, had hobbies and passions and sharp opinions on everything from the best sea food to who should be the city's next mayor. Instead of Clans, they organized in households loosely connected through alliances, and each of those worked to get some of its members placed in key positions. It sounded like a lot of very complex politics, and Horace lost track of half the stories shared with em about Festival betrayals, but e enjoyed the verve with which those were recounted to em, almost like fireside legends.

Soon, e grew comfortable mingling with the night-time crowd, sharing in their febrility as they watched the lights in the bay's dark water. Aliyah sometimes joined em, nodding along as e retold the many tales heard from residents about past Festivals.

Unfortunately, they weren't with em when the Archivist returned.

They appeared at the mouth of an alleyway, sunset turning their orange cape into a bright flare and the golden glitter of their mask into raging sparkles. Horace stared at them, eir heart rate scrambled from fear, until they bent into a partial bow and placed two fingers at the side of their forehead in what Horace thought was a greeting. E waved back, because e *always* waved at people, even mysterious strangers whose colleagues had a history of ruining eir day. In response, the Archivist gestured at em to follow.

This was a bad idea. E was alone, and this could be a trap of some sort. But e was almost a full hour from the Wagon, and when e didn't move, the Archivist stepped away, partly vanishing into the shadows of the alley. Horace jumped to eir feet.

"Wait!"

Horace ran after them.

5

The Sea Spirit's Guidance

The Archivist moved through the streets with ease, keeping ahead but always visible in a way that soon felt purposeful to Horace—like they were guiding em, rather than fleeing. E followed. Instead of worrying more with every step in the maze of alleys, Horace only became more determined. These people, these Archivists, they clearly knew more than they let on. This time e'd get answers—about Trenaze, about the Fragments, and about Aliyah.

The Archivist led em ever outward, keeping the Bay on their left, until they emerged at the edge of Alleaze. There was no dome to mark the end of the city, just a sudden lack of houses surrounding Horace, the street dying on a final structure: the broken base of a long-gone circular tower, its door cracked open, inviting. E'd come this far, so e pushed it the rest of the way and strode inside.

The building was a half-circle—a rarity in Alleaze's square architecture—the leftovers of an ancient home, about two stories tall at its highest. The curve of the arms reminded Horace of the cliffs enclosing the Bay, each reaching into the sea. Huge nets had been hung on the walls as decoration, and an isolated sleeping place had been arranged under the sole piece of remaining ceiling. Across from it were four work tables, with a full complement of tools that'd no doubt impress Rumi. In the distance, far afield and out of Alleaze proper, visible through the broken wall, Horace caught eir first glimpse of Fragments since arriving.

"Do you know what this place is?"

The voice dropped from above, its tone conversational and calm. Horace spun on emself to find the Archivist standing atop the broken wall, their cape snapping into the seaside wind. They cut a striking figure against the sunset sky, one hand on their hip and the other cast about in a grand gesture. Wasn't that the questions asked by the Archivist in the Dead Archives, too? It'd only been a set up to be pompous and cruel to Horace, and e didn't have the patience for it today.

"Of course not," e said. "You dragged me here, so I assume you do. Will you tell me, or is being mysterious and coy part of the Archivist vocation?"

Eir heart squeezed with the retort, memories of eir encounter in the Dead Archives a stark reminder that these were dangerous people. The Archivist then had been faster than even Keza, and Horace half-expected to find emself on eir ass for daring to talk back.

"We do have a flair for the dramatics," the Archivist replied with an apologetic bow, "but in this case, the answer is public knowledge, and no secret for me to keep. It is a shrine to the Sea Spirit—one of seven forming a ring around

Alleaze, and the one dedicated to craftsfolk."

"Is that one of their clans?" Horace asked.

"Not quite a clan here, but it is a path the Sea Spirit can guide locals to."

This must be the one represented by the net, if the aesthetic choices here were any indication. Horace had seen the same symbols repeated over and over throughout the Festival, and after eir numerous chats with the locals, e'd pieced together that they depicted the Sea Spirit's vocations. What e didn't understand was why this Archivist wanted to talk about it. It was unsettling, but e liked it far better than the arrogant aggressivity of the other one.

"You Archivists know a lot, don't you?" Horace asked.

Eir curiosity seeped through the question so strongly it overtook the bitterness of eir last encounter with them. E'd never been good with grudges, and e craved to discover who these people were, what they knew, and how they'd learned what they did to begin with.

Standing at the top of their wall, the Archivist

laughed. It was a musical sound, each chuckle flowing into the next, a melody of its own. The wind snapped their cape, and they bowed deeply. "We know everything and nothing at all, as is the nature of learning."

Horace wasn't sure what that was supposed to mean. "I don't understand. How does one know nothing and everything at once?"

"Well… Let me give you an example." They sat down in one graceful movement, legs dangling over the edge, their hooves clacking against the stone wall. "You arrived at Alleaze and learned that they had a Festival. What did it provoke in you?"

That was easy. "Excitement!"

E thought e heard a chortled laugh from the Archivist. "And?"

This time, Horace had to stop to ponder. "I wanted to participate. To … to know what it was like?"

"So you knew of a Festival, but had questions—questions about everything you didn't know yet."

"Oh! Because I knew nothing about it!"

The Archivist leaned forward, and Horace wondered if they had the same smirk under their gold-specked mask as it sported. "Exactly. Everything you learn is a lesson in what you don't know yet."

Trenaze had a saying about this, or close to: a master is but an apprentice who understands what they must still learn. E'd never thought of it as knowing *everything and nothing*, but this Archivist had already admitted to enjoying the dramatic. At least they were nice! Maybe Horace would get more than cryptic threats and reproach out of them. And e was going to be clever about it, too.

"Then tell me your name, so I can grasp everything I don't know about you."

It drew a pleased exclamation out of them. Victory!

"You will need to be satisfied with Archivist Kol, I'm afraid. Any pronouns would do, but these days I am particularly fond of he/him."

He placed his hands on either side of him, set

his hooves against the stone wall, and pushed himself off, leaping the entire two floors down to the ground and landing with a grace that sharply reminded Horace to stay wary of these people. When he spoke again, his voice had dropped low.

"Are those the questions you should be asking?"

Fear jolted through Horace. Of course they weren't! Did e have a limited number? Was e wasting time? All of a sudden, *who* this Archivist was seemed far less important—or rather, less pressing. Horace still wanted to know. E would always want to know, if only out of personal curiosity. But if e had to wait, that was all right.

"Your colleague called Aliyah the Hero," e blurted.

Kol tilted his head to the side. "That is not a question."

Horace huffed, flustered. E hadn't had time to make it one! "What-what did that mean?"

"That they're destined for grand things, I suppose. Saving people, saving worlds—who knows?" A minute shrug shook his shoulders, and he began walking around Horace, tracing circles within the tower. "There are all kinds of heroes. Big ones, small ones … tragic ones, even, though where I'm from, we don't speak of those."

Again, Horace found emself struggling to parse through what that meant, at least for Aliyah. E did not want to think about *tragic*, not after the first Archivist had said. "The other Archivist—"

"Neomi," Kol provided, before letting Horace go on.

"They said 'the world' couldn't afford a mistake. That didn't sound small!" Belatedly, e realized that wasn't a question either, so e added. "Is-is it related to the Fragments? Do you know what they are?"

Kol stopped, and his hoof tapped the ground twice. "I do not know of the Fragments."

Horace pouted. Was he lying? Horace had never been good at determining that. Disappointment burned in eir stomach and e blurted "That's not very helpful."

"Ah! My apologies." He did not sound sorry. "Here is my first piece of advice, then: when you tell people they are a Hero, it changes them and changes the story. It can spoil it."

Of course their first suggestion would be to keep a secret! Horace crossed eir arm. "Aliyah deserves to know."

Kol also crossed his arms, and Horace had the distinct impression the mimicry was on purpose. "Do they? It is a lot of pressure, to think of one's self as responsible for the world's fate. Foisting this upon them now is not the kindness you believe. But, perhaps more importantly, is it relevant, what they deserve, when the impact is the same?"

Horace wanted to protest—eir guts still said it was, but e couldn't quite wrap eir mind around Kol's words. E'd need to think about them, and the way the Archivist's natural playful tone had vanished with them.

"Stories matter, Horace." He turned towards the wide field beyond, then hopped onto the lower trail of the broken-down wall. "You learn a lot, listening to them and how they change. For example, my home has many stories of a Sea Spirit, but it didn't live underwater. It flew the sky, and some said it could ride through any storm. Isn't it curious that even at the bottom of the Almari Bay, it still needs to catch lightning?"

It was strange, but Horace didn't know what e was supposed to draw from that. "I don't understand."

"Neither do I," he said, "but I can't help but think the answer to that mystery is on the bay's seafloor, accessible only to those who can breathe underwater."

Underwater? Horace *still* didn't understand why they were even talking about this, but as e fumbled for eir next question, Kol touched the edge of his mask in what *must* have been a salutation. Then he leaped off his wall, vanishing on the other side of the tower. By the time Horace had run out, he was nowhere to be found.

"You followed him to talk *alone*?"

In the end, Horace had told everyone about Archivist Kol the moment e'd returned to the Wagon. There was no point trying to hide it: e was still agitated, and Aliyah had taken one look at eir face before inviting em to share with a quiet "Horace?"

So the entire crew had settled in the main space: Aliyah and Rumi at the table, Keza on her usual rafter, and Horace on the two-seater. E'd begun eir tale slowly and hadn't gotten very far before Rumi interrupted em with his question.

"I was far from the Wagon, and I didn't want to lose him again!" Horace protested. "He was very friendly, all things considered."

"You couldn't have known that ahead of time," Rumi pointed out. "What if he hadn't been? What if you'd disappeared, or he'd led you to Fragments, or-or—"

"But he did not," Aliyah cut in. "We can debate better safety or communication once Horace has finished."

No one stopped em a second time. E tried not

to forget anything—the chase through Alleaze's streets, the shrine dedicated to craftsfolk, the strange discussion about knowledge and stories, and how e'd gotten names for the two Archivists—Kol and Neomi. Horace knew which one was eir favourite, that was for sure.

The more e talked, the more e realized how little e'd truly learned. E'd been so caught up in the moment, the quick turns of conversations and the hundred questions bouncing in eir heads, e'd not absorbed what e was being told—or not told.

Then there was the matter of what Horace had been asked *not* to share.

It had eaten at em all the way back, this idea that it was better for Aliyah *not* to tell them that all these Archivists considered them a hero, that it'd come with a pressure that could be destructive. E had a hard time imagining what it was like, for anyone to expect great things out of you. It had always been the reverse for em: mentors had expected Horace to fail, and e'd inevitably conformed to it.

Perhaps, Horace had thought, that wasn't so different. It had all added up to so much pressure to make the next apprenticeship work, to prove that e was capable, that e was worth something. It had made em miserable, even through the upbeat optimism, and e'd only begun to realize how much the longer e stayed in the Wagon. Here, they marvelled at eir experimental dinner plans, eager to test anything e came up with, trusting em to mostly manage, and what did it matter if e'd forgotten the boiling water until it evaporated that one time? They cheered as e trained with Keza every morning, gathering bruises as e painstakingly mastered better reflexes and balance. They indulged eir obsession for games, all too excited to play themselves, everyone settling into a healthy competition as they learned each other's quirks. The Wagon made Horace feel like e didn't need to *try* to belong, e simply did.

It can spoil them. That's what Kol had said. That it'd spoil what they had, rot it to its core. What if telling Aliyah about the whole Hero thing made them feel like they didn't belong *as is*, that they should become more? Or that others around needed to be better, competent in ways Horace had never been? When Kol had first said it changed things, Horace hadn't understood how, or why, but the more e'd thought about it, the more worried e got, and when e reached that part of the conversation, eir stomach had knotted itself up very tight. E didn't want to say, but e couldn't *not* say anything either, and that left em very confused as to what was the right thing to do at all. E would have to try, though.

"I asked about Fragments, and why they were so weird around Aliyah, because last time the first Archivist had sounded so informed. But Kol didn't. He said he didn't know anything about Fragments."

It earned em a snort from Keza, whose tail flicked in obvious derision. "You believed him?"

Horace had. E couldn't explain why, but e trusted Kol. Maybe it was the friendliness, or the music in his laughter, but under the mask and verbal deflection, he'd seemed honest. Neomi had been honest, too; they'd just been a jerk.

"He sounded frustrated," e said as justification. "I think he wanted to know."

Neither Rumi nor Keza appeared particularly convinced. Aliyah had retreated into their thoughtful expression, the one e still had difficulty reading. Slowly absorbing, mulling, turning things over in their mind.

"What I do not understand," they started after a moment, "is why they spoke with you at all. Why send us an Archivist to say so little? Or did he come of his own volition?"

"Maybe he was lonely?" Horace suggested, and when faced with everyone's obvious doubts, e added, "He did mention something about the Sea Spirit, too! Apparently, there are more legends about it and it can fly through storms! He seemed to think it was very strange for it to be underwater, but I don't understand why. It's the *Sea* Spirit, not the Sky Spirit."

"Sounds like he's full of shit," Keza said, before rolling off the rafters and dropping down in the middle of them. "Why does it matter, what Mystery Mask thought he was doing? All we gotta do is wait for the lights to keep popping up, get on a big wooden floater, and cross the ocean—then we'll be rid of them, yeah?"

"One can hope," Rumi mumbled. "You can all continue speculating, but I've got work to do. I suspect we sail on the *Pegasus* no matter who earns it, so I'll be in the workshop drawing plans for modifications. Hopefully we can pay with them." He slid down his chair, then turned to Horace, waggling a finger. "And Horace? Stop following noted jerks into dingy streets in cities you're unfamiliar with."

Horace opened eir mouth to protest as Rumi walked away—Kol *hadn't* been a jerk!—but thought better of it. He'd just tell em *again* that e'd had no way of knowing that ahead of time, and he was right. Instead, e grinned at Rumi's back.

"The next time he shows up, I'll invite him over then!"

Rumi's hand stalled in the curtains to his workshop, and he half-turned, looking over his shoulder with a sharp, hostile hiss. "The Wagon's off-limits!"

Horace pouted. Even though e'd mostly meant it as a tease, e'd gotten attached to the idea the moment it had crossed eir lips.

In the end, the point became moot, as Archivist Kol remained nowhere to be seen for the following days, and the fifth light appeared in the depths of the Bay, signalling the full closure of all trades and the next phase of the Festival. Horace continued to find small gatherings to join, and although e was disappointed Kol didn't show up again, even as a distant onlooker, e enjoyed the time spent with locals.

One by one, under the supervision of a select few acolytes from the last cycle, the people of Alleaze sought the Sea Spirit's guidance, received their role, and returned to their alliances to discuss how to use the remaining tokens to get important members in key position. The stories Horace heard as e shared benches, tree trunks, and crates with strangers by the waterfront changed from their hopes and dreams to either triumphs or disappointment, depending on the Sea Spirit's whims. E saw Valetta again, who'd not been granted the civil servant role she'd desired, but one as a craftsperson. She was working with her alliance to be assigned in textiles, which she loved and had handled two cycles ago.

With every passing day, the tension in the city increased. It weighed on casual conversations, a crackling energy of anticipation Horace couldn't place. Shouldn't the knowledge of their appointed vocations be a source of relief for the people in Alleaze? Rumi had certainly seemed far less on edge once they'd learned Jameela had received a sailor role and could try to land captainship of the *Pegasus*. Why wasn't everyone in the city slowly releasing the breath so clearly held while they waited for the fifth light to blink into existence?

Their tension seeped into the Wagon crew: Keza had less tolerance in her swimming lessons, giving up faster, Aliyah laughed less during their nightly games and retreated more often to a world of their own, sitting on the roof and practising their transformation, and Rumi spent longer isolated in his workshop—until they exceeded the thirty days Jameela had estimated, and his patience ran out. Horace watched him stomp out of the Wagon one morning, heading directly towards the docks, so e followed and they roamed it until they found Jameela.

The ex-but-perhaps-future Captain had been lounging with two other sailors when they arrived, trading herbs for their respective pipes. Each had a differently shaped one, going from a long thin stick to Jameela's deep, curved yellow one, and Jameela had been in a heated argument about the merit of pepperoot in her mix of herbs. When she spotted the two of them, she split from the group.

"Need help?"

Rumi's tail flicked, rattling across the ground's pebbles. "Coming for news. It's been well over thirty days, and we gave you what we had. Shouldn't this be finished now? Can't you negotiate for the *Pegasus'* captainship proper? What are we waiting for?"

"No one negotiates before the sixth light," Jameela said. "It brings misfortune on your alliance to do so before the Sea Spirit has guided everyone."

"It tells you when it's done, I hope."

"With the sixth light," Jameela repeated, a hint of annoyance to their voice. "By all accounts, it should be soon. There are few left who have not received their guidance. Cool your wheels, Master Rumi. There is nothing you can do to speed the process."

That didn't please Rumi, who spent the walk back devising methods to locate and drag every missing Alleazan to their guidance, drawing a number of curious glances. While he did not put any of these plans into action, everyone in Alleaze did, in time, find their way to the Sea Spirit's guidance.

The sixth light, however, had still not lit up.

Speculation ran wild in the seaside gatherings. Guesses that someone was missing were countered by older folks pointing out someone was *always* missing, and the Sea Spirit moved on regardless. Many wondered if the spirit was sick, or lost, or confused, but since the people with acolyte roles had not negotiated precise positions, no one knew whom to consult for answers, exactly. Through it all, more and more of the residents turned away from Horace, physically excluding em from conversations, and mutterings about the dangers of including outsiders reached eir ears. Horace stopped going, limiting eir time out of the Wagon to the increasingly infrequent swimming sessions with Keza.

Thirty-nine days after their arrival—Rumi had made a point of counting—they were hailed from outside as the four of them shared a quiet and tense breakfast.

"Honoured Strangers! We need to discuss important matters."

Horace recognized the deep voice; this was Adelar Hilstorm, the munonoxi who'd run the hammer-and-clam game over a month ago. They exchanged a quick glance, then Keza looked at the ceiling before climbing the ladder to the roof, grabbing her staff on the way. Horace, Rumi, and Aliyah instead left by the front door.

Outside, Adelar waited for them, his rainbow tunic replaced by equally colourful pants and a deep, plunging shirt that revealed a muscular body covered in a dark fuzz. *That* would have been considered very enticing in Trenaze, as well as a dangerous game to play with the sun. Maybe the etiquette here was different? The sun did spend a lot of time hidden behind clouds, even on days it didn't rain.

Fanned out behind him stood four others, and by the leather arm guards and the spears on their backs, Horace expected them to serve a similar role as Clan Zestra.

"We are here," Aliyah said.

Adelar bowed his head in salutation, then stomped the ground with an awkward sigh. Although he retained a lot of the presence he'd exhibited a month ago, calling people to his Storm Catcher challenge, the full showmanship persona had given way to a man more ill at ease.

"This is quite irregular, and I am not entirely

comfortable with my role in it, but I hope you will not see my acceptance of it despite the sixth light's absence as disrespect to the Sea Spirit's necessary meditation time."

"Oh! Are you doing something before it got negotiated?" Horace asked. "Jameela said that could bring you misfortune. Please don't do that on our account!"

All five Alleazans turned to the Bay and touched their shoulders briefly, a sign Horace had come to know as either a prayer, or a warding. Maybe e shouldn't have mentioned the bad luck.

"Unfortunately, I am, indeed, filling my old role as the Sea Spirit's voice in the city." He snapped his hoof on the ground again, as if to chase away the uneasiness.

"Alleaze has undergone the Sea Spirit's guidance—all of Alleaze. We have asked every alliance, gone door to door to those who remain independent, and every citizen has received its role from the Sea Spirit."

That's what everyone had been saying, too,

and Horace had a sense e was about to get an answer to much of the overheard speculation.

"But?" Aliyah asked, their voice soft but firm.

"The Sea Spirit has not chosen a Storm Catcher."

6

Underwater Mysteries

They were brought to the Sea Spirit's Altar—the glow of gold and teal visible every night at the bottom of the bay, an underwater glass bubble Horace had marvelled at from a distance ever since Valetta had first pointed out its existence.

Adelar had led them to the northern shore of Alleaze, past the docks and to a beautiful park with benches carved to look like the colourful coral formations in the bay. At the end had been a gate made of several archways of chiselled sandstone with veins of a lovely turquoise worked throughout, each arch lower than the previous one as they framed a stairwell down.

The path within had an eerie quality to it, its sandstone walls and floors interlaced with half-broken steel beams upon which crawled a thick, grey sediment. At times, an entire section of the wall became luxurious wood panelling, and sometimes it was the ground under eir feet that changed to a plush carpet. The mismatched tunnel made em feel as if e was slowly being transported into another world, and e'd forgotten all about the long stairs downward until their surroundings turned to glass and the bay opened up above and around them.

They stood in an underwater bubble—quarter bubble, really, since it was cut by the floor and another opulent wood façade. Blue lights hung from the ceiling, casting an eerie glow all around, creating the illusion of floating in water. There were no seats here, no furniture to speak of, nothing of note but the shifting colour of the bay overhead, the occasional curious fish, and the ominous carving in the dark wooden wall.

It depicted an elegant creature, with a long, scaled body and fluttery fins forming a crest like waves along it. Towards its neck, however, the body lost its scales and instead had … feathers? It was hard to tell, as the art piece had been worn down through time, but Horace thought the ridges looked like strange wings. The head was rounder than most lizards', sported a sharp and pointed beak, and it emerged from the wall almost threateningly. The upper half of its beak curled all the way around, forming a curved receptacle. The end of the body also jutted out of the fresque, spiralling in a conic shape and leaving a hole large enough for Horace's arm. A slide had been carved into it.

Of the four guards that had flanked them during the entire walk, two remained, on each side of the entrance. Adelar, who had stayed a step ahead, split farther from the group and turned to face them.

"Welcome, Honoured Strangers, to the Sea Spirit Altar."

"Full offence," Keza said, "but this is bullshit."

"It is duly noted, Master Keza, but

unfortunately we see no other way."

"So you brought us here … to get the Sea Spirit's guidance?" Rumi asked. "Are we not allowed to leave? Did we sign some sort of blood oath when we played that first game with you?"

"In truth, I could not say," Adelar replied. "None of us foresaw this, and we welcomed you to the Festival in good faith, as it has never to our knowledge caused problems. If we ask that you receive the guidance now, it is out of necessity. Alleaze needs a Storm Catcher, and we must discover if the Sea Spirit has chosen one of you. The possibility pleases no one."

"Didn't stop you from bringing the whole militia," Rumi grumbled. "But whatever, we'll play this last game if it'll get us moving. We put a token in?"

"One would normally slip as many tokens as they'd desire on the Sea Spirit's tail, then press one of the buttons located on its rings to express its wish. I have, however, been given to understand that you no longer have the tokens you've earned, so we've prepared one for each of you." His tone was tight, filled with obvious disapproval, but it seemed that was the extent to which Adelar would comment on their little deal with Jameela. He reached into his pants' deep pockets and retrieved four tokens. "Insert it, and the Sea Spirit will return your role."

"Shame we can't tell it to leave us alone," Keza said.

Horace understood their resentment, but e couldn't bring emself to be angry about Alleaze's decision to drag them here. This place was a marvel in itself, and the prospect of participating excited em. E wished it hadn't been under the implicit threat of the guards. They made em feel sad, not unlike the pang of regret when e spilled beet juice on eir favourite clothes. Something had been ruined, and it was too late to change anything about it.

"If only we'd come here under different circumstances," Horace said. "It's so beautiful."

Adelar bowed to em in acknowledgement, but did not apologize. They all seemed very convinced of this, and Horace wondered why they stayed so polite about it. None of eir Clan Zestra training had involved etiquette around strong-arming outsiders into your local faith, unfortunately.

Rumi mumbled something about getting on with it, and stretched on the tip of his clawed toes to slip a token in the slide. Despite his foul mood, his tail twitched with anticipation as the token rolled inside and clinked within. He leaned forward and touched the carved fresco, his head tilted towards it. A strange, off-key whistling emerged from the Sea Spirit, the notes jumping from low to high with little semblance of melody, and a loud clank interrupted it again. The seconds of silence that followed had to be some of the most drawn-out Horace had ever experienced.

A flat, polished rock rolled out of the beak along the inside of its curve and came to rest on the receptacle carved into its end. Rumi hopped to grab it, then held it up. A long scroll had been carved into it, its outlines inked in black. Horace had seen this symbol hundreds of times in the last month.

"Civil servant," Adelar declared. "You are not our Storm Catcher."

"I'm not your anything," Rumi countered, shoving the rock back in Adelar's hands. "Someone else can go now."

"I can go," Horace chirped.

Eir enthusiasm caused both Rumi and Keza to stare at em, part confusion and part betrayal. Oops. E couldn't help it! E wanted to know what the Sea Spirit thought of em, what would have been eir role—eir vocation—had it been decided for em. The excitement turned into anxiety as e approached and set the token in the tail. Would e have found eir place, had e not had to undergo the trials of the apprenticeships e picked, or would the struggles have remained, unfit to fulfill the Sea Spirit's plans? Eir hands hovered above the rings allowing em to indicate a preference, only to retreat after a moment. E wanted to know the Sea Spirit's opinion, undiluted and unobstructed.

If the clinks and clanks and strange music had seemed long for Rumi, they became excruciating for em. E worked up a sweat, and the thumps of eir heart turned painful, a sharp stab at the inside of eir chest. All eir life, e'd struggled to figure out who e was, to find eir place in eir world. But here on this distant bay, e could offer a strange token to the Sea Spirit, listen to haunting and discordant notes, and watch a smooth pebble roll out of a beak, and e had eir answer.

E stared at it now, hesitant to pick it up and see what had been carved into it. It felt as if eir entire world hinged on the answer, even though e knew it meant nothing, not unless the stone showed Storm Catcher. Slowly, steadying emself with a deep breath, Horace reached for the stone and flipped it over.

It was blank.

Nothing carved on its surface, no trace of ink or any symbol. No role for em.

"A choice," Adelar said. "Few are granted such trust by the Sea Spirit and allowed to fill the role they deem best."

"But…"

E had *wanted* an answer. E'd had the choice all eir life and e'd never known what to do with it.

This felt like a betrayal. Just this once, Horace had hoped someone else would tell em who e was, someone who could read an entire population and quite certainly eir own simple mind.

A clank brought em back to the present, and e looked up to see Keza holding a stone with a fishing spear on it.

"Fishing?" she said, brow furrowed.

"Sailor, which does indeed include fishing. It's a common role and the foundation of life in the Bay."

"Sure is a blessing I'm not living here, then."

Adelar didn't acknowledge the rebuttal. E had turned towards Aliyah, the last of them who had not received the Sea Spirit's guidance. The guards that had accompanied them shuffled, awkward.

"I suppose it would be fitting," Adelar said. "Shall I tell you again the story of the Storm Catcher?"

Aliyah's lips twitched into a smile. "If your theory holds, I will need to finish the tale for you."

They stepped forward and put the token in,

and silence returned as they listened once more to the haunting melody of the Sea Spirit's guidance. The notes echoed in their underwater chamber, and Horace could have sworn they had changed, their tune higher pitched, faster, and more upbeat.

They're destined for grand things, I suppose. Saving people, saving worlds. Archivist Kol's words hung at the edge of eir mind, bringing a deep sense of foreboding.

The stone rolled out, and unlike all others, it was pure black. Whispers ran through the onlooking militia as Aliyah stepped forward and picked it up. A golden lightning bolt had been carved on its upside. The Storm Catcher.

"I suppose this story is my story," Aliyah said, staring at the coin.

The hitch in their voice snagged at Horace's mind. E snapped to attention as eir friend closed their fingers around the stone. *This story is my story* wasn't a coincidental phrasing. Whenever Aliyah had faced Fragments—whenever they had absorbed them, vaporizing the sharp golden shards into mist and soaking it in—they had declared similar words, pounded them into the world with the force of an incantation.

"You sure, Aliyah?" Rumi asked. "They can say what they want about rituals and shit, but we can ditch this town and travel all the way north to Ferneze. They've got ocean carriers too."

The suggestion sent an angry ripple through the militia, though Adelar did not flinch. Aliyah shook their head. "Thank you, Rumi, but I can accept this role, provided we are guaranteed passage on the *Pegasus*, with Captain Jameela at its command."

"I'm afraid a place on the *Pegasus* might be only possible for your company, Storm Catcher," Adelar warned.

"Listen here, hammer-man," Keza started.

Adelar raised a hand and snapped a hoof to interrupt her. "It pains me, I assure you," he said, voice as firm and cordial as always, "but in Alleaze's history, no Storm Catcher has ever survived the ritual. I would know. My own brother was the last one chosen by the Sea Spirit."

In the deafening silence that followed, panic shot through Horace. No one had ever survived? They wanted Aliyah to die for them, a ritual sacrifice to their Sea Spirit, and they hadn't even warned them that this was the risk they ran, accepting guidance from it? All of a sudden, the armed company seemed far more sinister.

This is not your tale, and you will surely die for it. That's what Archivist Neomi had told em, all these weeks ago, in the Dead Archives. Maybe they'd been right all along. If Alleaze needed a sacrifice… Eir palm curled around eir blank stone, and e stepped forward, between Adelar and Aliyah.

"I'll do it," e declared. "I'll be your Storm Catcher."

Adelar was already shaking his head. "You were not chosen by the Sea Spirit."

"But it told me to pick my own path!" E turned around and grabbed one of Aliyah's small, dark hands into eir own, bigger and paler. "It doesn't have to be you."

"Horace." They met their gaze, voice firm and

warm. "I am touched by your volunteering, but I will not relinquish my role to send you to your death. Not when I can survive it."

But Adelar had just said…

As e fumbled to understand Aliyah's confidence, they turned back towards the munonoxi. "You have your Storm Catcher. When my storm is here, you know where to find me."

At the first step they took towards the exit, the armed guards blocked the path. Adelar hadn't moved, or frowned, or even flinched. Their opaque patience was beginning to grate on Horace.

"The Storm Catcher, once chosen, is brought in isolation, to better commune with the Sea Spirit and prepare themself. You should make your goodbyes. The storm never dawdles."

"It will need dawdle a night, as will your preparations." Aliyah tilted their chin up, and ice filled their voice. "My acceptance is not permission for you to order me around, regardless of how many spears you command. I *will* spend this day and night with my people, in our Wagon home. Guard *that*, if you must."

Adelar and Aliyah remained locked onto one another, and the air within the Sea Spirit Altar became so charged, Horace half-expected the storm to erupt then and there. Then Adelar bowed deeply and made a sweeping gesture towards the exit. The two guards stepped aside.

"We will seek you in the morning, Storm Catcher."

Aliyah left without another word, and they all followed. Keza hissed at the militia on her way out, and Horace suspected she could've knocked them down if she'd wanted, even without her staff in hand to begin with.

Aliyah dragged them to the exit. Adelar and his guards remained a respectable distance behind until they climbed the stairs and into the park, to find hundreds of locals gathered amongst the flower beds. They fell silent when the group emerged then parted into two, a wave of body giving way for them. Aliyah stopped sharply, and Horace bumped into them. E put a hand on their shoulder, hoping to reassure.

As they struggled to get their bearings, Adelar swooped in front of them and spread his arms out.

"Residents of Alleaze, my peers, colleagues, friends, and rivals, the Sea Spirit has chosen its Storm Catcher!"

He grabbed Aliyah's hand and yanked it up, provoking a wave of relieved cheers from the crowd. Aliyah tensed and leaned against Horace's chest, but other than that they faced the crowd with their chin raised, allowing for a few seconds of celebration before slipping their hand out of Adelar's grip. Everyone stared, perhaps waiting on Aliyah to speak, but they moved on. Horace, Rumi, and Keza all fell into step around them, a protective guard in case anyone tried something. Horace had no idea what they could even attempt, but it was clear Aliyah wanted to vanish from sight as fast as possible, and e intended to make it happen.

The crowd thankfully thinned quickly, and they made their way through the winding streets to the Wagon.

They piled inside, and Horace set water to boil and rummaged through their cupboards for some simple snacks to put together. They hadn't properly restocked since arriving in the city, choosing local eateries instead, but they did have a bag of dried apple slices coated with salt and an as-of-yet unidentified, ochre spice that burned eir tongue and had this fun, almost acidic aftertaste. Horace threw those in a bowl, set it in the centre, and turned to Aliyah.

"Talk to us," e said.

What e *wanted* to say was "you're not going alone. I won't let you die. You don't have to do this. I'm not sure who I'd be without you" but the words had caught in eir throat, blocked by fear of their reception. E hadn't told Aliyah about the Archivists dubbing them a Hero, or that they saw in them something special, the same way the Sea Spirit had. E should, e really should, but then e'd have to mention how e'd sworn emself to them, how *your story is my story* had been a call to em, too, and e was afraid it'd break the simplicity of what they had. It felt like *too much*, and in Horace's long history of apprenticeships, "you're doing too much" had more often been criticism than praise, a rebuttal to eir earnestness. E didn't want to be too much to Aliyah.

"The Sea Spirit is a Fragment, or an amalgam of them," Aliyah said.

Rumi froze with an apple sliced halfway into his mouth, then set the thing back down. "Nah, I think it's just a machine," he said. "You can hear it turning. Not sure what's in the belly of the beast, but it's not some benevolent spirit."

Aliyah was shaking their head long before he finished. "I sensed it, Rumi, and perhaps more importantly, it sensed me. Would a machine have withheld its Storm Catcher rune until I approached? Or do you truly think I'm *that* unlucky."

"That *was* weird as shit," Keza agreed. "The whole place is, if you ask me. If that's how the rest of the world is, I can see why the Elders want to keep it far away from the village."

"Like your home wasn't full of creeps," Rumi muttered. His words were soon followed by a sharp yelp as Keza kicked him under the table.

Horace rolled eir eyes at their banter, but eir attention hadn't truly left Aliyah. They stared at their hands, lips pressed into a thin line, a whole universe of hidden emotions swirling in their dark eyes.

"So the lights, the roles, everything ... you think it's Fragments? Is that not too organized for them?"

"I do not know." They sighed and finally met Horace's gaze. "All I know is that I felt them, and if this is their way of calling to me, then should I not respond?"

"No!" E reached across the table to grab their hand, knocking the bowl of dried apples. Keza caught it before it could tip over. "Listen, I don't understand what those Fragments want, or are, but it can't be anything good. What if they possessed past Storm Catchers, or drowned them? Or-or you'll do your thing, and collapse, and then no one will be there to help and—"

"Horace," Aliyah interrupted, voice soft but firm. They looked at em, and as the seconds stretched, their lips curled into an ever-wider smile. "I do not wish to die in this town. I want to reach the grove that haunts my dreams, to know what it means and why I am what I am. But solving this is the way forward, the same way unblocking the Inari Pass was."

"We did that together," Horace said.

Aliyah's smile vanished. "They did not seem inclined to let two of us go. But I promise you, I can handle this. I can handle anything if I know you will watch over me after."

The games of saira they played that night had a melancholy layer to them Horace could never quite shake. E chose eir painted dice with care, trying harder than usual to offer Aliyah a good challenge, eir inevitable loss to their ruthlessness notwithstanding. They laughed and ate well, and seemed relaxed despite the incoming trials, and that was all Horace could ask for. E held tighter that night, and hoped they dreamed of their fantastical world of flying ships and magical crystals, and not of Fragments drowning them in the Almari Bay.

Aliyah's departure from the Wagon was marked with very few words, and a background cheer from the city celebrating the illumination of the sixth light. In a strange twist of fate, they declared, the Sea Spirit had favoured the outsiders and a Storm Catcher had been found.

All Aliyah had said was "I will see you soon."

Their absence left a growing void within Horace. E stood on the top platform, staring at the fluffy white clouds in the sky, wondering how fast they would turn into dark, looming grey ones. Keza let em off the training hook—eirs and hers—and brought em deep-fried fish to eat once she realized e'd had neither breakfast nor lunch. It felt wrong, to be here waiting for Aliyah to participate in the city's ritual sacrifice. E had promised to protect them, but what could e do? E'd need to be there with them, to—

I can't help to think the answer to that mystery is

at the bottom of the bay, accessible only to those who can breathe underwater.

The Archivist had known. Kol, who'd come to have a casual chat about the Sea Spirit legends, who'd told them directly where e'd need to go. He'd known or guessed this would happen, and he'd tried to get Horace ready in time. To help.

Maybe it wasn't too late. E had to try. If there was one thing Horace had always done, it was to try even when it felt impossible. With one last glance at the bright waters of the bay, e rushed down the ladder and to Rumi's workshop.

E stopped at the edge, the curtain partly pulled and in eir hand, suddenly reluctant to interrupt. Rumi slid a minuscule wooden cog within his current project, mumbling to himself as he moved it little by little until it settled in with the most satisfying click. This was a toy, in theory, meant to spring up very high. Horace could see two frog-like legs still on the table, no doubt to be added once Rumi had figured out all the inside stuff.

"Rumi," e finally said, unable to contain emself any longer.

Rumi yelped and spun about as if caught red-handed in the middle of a crime. He must have been *very* absorbed in his work!

"Horace, what are the workshop rules?" he hissed.

"No-no talking while you work," Horace muttered. "But you're always tinkering and I need your help."

Rumi set his wrench down and leaned against his workshop's high table. "Maybe there's a reason I'm always working. Maybe it's to keep Keza from poking fun at me all day long, or you from petitioning for another game. Maybe these little toys are what gets us a warmer welcome in most cities, and I'm working hard for everyone's sake."

Maybe, Horace thought, he was also being particularly snippy because he couldn't help Aliyah either. He'd been like that with protecting the Wagon before.

"I-I understand that, but Rumi, you're the genius. I need you to make me a water-breathing machine. Before the storm. You can do that, can't you?"

The annoyed twitches of Rumi's tail had stopped at "genius" and he preened under the compliment—until the full request registered, and he hissed at Horace. "Sure, Horace! I can work miracles, even impossible contraptions on impossible deadlines. A water-breathing machine!"

He threw his small arms up, and his high seat spun with the movement. Horace's stomach sank all the way into eir heels. If Rumi couldn't do this, then how could e investigate the waters? How could e keep Aliyah safe?

"I can't give up on them, Rumi. Please. Kol thought there was something at the bottom—a mystery to solve."

Rumi's small shoulders slumped in defeat and the sarcasm drained out of him. "I get it, big fella, but I—"

He stopped short, his hand slapping on his workbench and his eyes rolling up, almost completely disappearing. Horace stepped forward, half-expecting him to collapse and fall

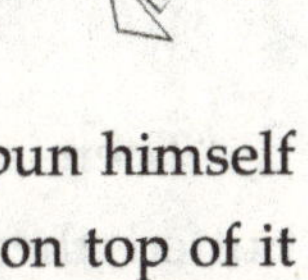

down the chair, but instead Rumi spun himself to face the table and half-scrambled on top of it to grab parchments and pencils. He scribbled furiously, small arms flailing as he drew a hundred lines on his big sheet, sketching out tubes and other weird contraptions before scrapping it all and starting again. Horace had never seen anything like this frenzy. Rumi had forgotten him, absorbed in his confusing work, muttering feverishly.

As suddenly as it had begun, Rumi stopped and slumped over his table. He heaved a long sigh, and the frantic snapping of his tail turned into a slow, lazy swing. Horace inched closer, and that seemed to catch his friend's attention. Rumi blinked, then stifled a yawn. He glanced at the large sheet on top of his renewed chaos, and Horace swore he looked surprised by it.

"I can do it," he said. "I don't know when I'll sleep, but unless the storm's tomorrow, I can manage."

Hope ballooned in Horace's chest. "Just like that?"

"There's nothing 'just like that' in it!" Rumi huffed, then grabbed one of the dozen pieces of paper scattered over his desk. "Now, these are all the materials I'll need, and we don't have any tokens left to pay for them. You figure it out. I have to start working."

In the end, Keza promised em she could get her hands on the full list, and Horace chose not to question through which methods. If it brought em at the bottom of the bay, e didn't care.

7

Catching the Lightning

The clouds gathered above had grown so dark the day felt like nighttime. They hung low, the air heavy from the weight of what they heralded and of Alleaze's building anticipation.

Five days had passed since Aliyah had left the Wagon to become Alleaze's Storm Catcher. Five days of waking up without them in eir arms. Five days without their silent presence in the Wagon, their quick wits or sudden burst of laughter, their light smile as they sat discreetly with Horace. It had felt like an eternity.

With Rumi engulfed in the water-breather project, Horace had no one but Keza to keep the loneliness away. They intensified the swimming lessons, and Horace often left her to practice without help to go dive deeper into the bay, accustoming eir body to the currents as best as e could. The increasingly large waves made it all the more interesting.

They also added evening battle training to their routine. Horace gathered new bruises every day, but e kept growing faster on eir feet, more aware of eir surroundings and how e could use them to eir advantage. The sword and shield no longer felt awkward in eir hands, and for all that Keza still slipped past eir defences, e had become better at getting into hers, too.

More importantly, however, e crawled into bed exhausted to the bone, which made it easier to forget about the missing warmth between eir arms, or how Aliyah would wake from their nightmares alone, with no one to hold them steady as they found their bearings and sank into slumber again.

After five days of promising emself e'd help Aliyah soon, Rumi completed his project. He emerged from the workshop jittery from the lack of sleep, his shoulders stooped and his tail slow to flick about, but pride shone in his eyes.

"Another miracle performed by Rumi of the Wonderful Wares!" Then they stepped outside, and he noticed the darkened clouds. "Don't think we'll have much time for extensive testing. That's a storm coming if I ever saw one."

The skies agreed with a distant rumble.

Horace wanted to make it down there before Aliyah. E had cornered Adelar once and bombarded him with questions about the ritual, but all e'd gotten as an answer was that the Storm Catcher entered the Bay at the first crack of lightning, and that Alleaze would gather on the choppy waters to witness their sacrifice. Only a handful of tiny ships floated in the bay so far, each with small awnings deployed to keep the drizzling rain out. Horace doubted it'd be enough when it turned into a downpour.

By the time Horace, Rumi, and Keza had rowed their own probably stolen boat in the bay, a dozen more embarkations had joined the early crew. They kept their distance, hoping no one would notice Horace undressing.

"Are you listening to me?" Rumi asked.

Horace snapped back to the conversation at hand. Rumi *had* been talking. He was holding up his water breather, a strange cylinder attached to a full-face mask. "Yes, yes!"

"Then what did I just say?"

Horace stared at him, lips parted and mind empty. "Erm…"

Rumi clacked his teeth. "I've not had a lick of sleep to build you this thing, and I won't have you break it because you can't focus for two seconds. I said: you can't pull at this once I get it in place. Crouch down."

Horace obeyed, and the boat rocked under them. Keza gripped each side with a hiss while Rumi pushed on his tiptoes and passed the big mask over eir drenched curls. He then climbed on Horace's back and finagled with the straps behind eir head, tightening the mask. On occasions, he stopped to prod at the lining between the apparatus and Horace's face, checking that it was properly sealed. It was hot, to breathe in this thing.

"Right. I already put air in this tank," Rumi patted the cylinder attached against Horace's back. "It's a fair amount of it. Two hours, maybe a bit less? Lots more than it looks, anyway. Right now, you're not using it at all. When you need it, you pull this lever." He grabbed Horace's hand and led it to the correct lever. "Try to hold your breath often and conserve. This is all brand-new stuff."

"So your calculations could be wrong, or you could have tinkered something off, and e could run out while at the bottom of the bay," Keza pointed out.

Rumi's tail swiped behind him as he turned around. "E won't! It's a prototype, but I trust it! It's some of my finest work."

"And you're functioning on *fumes* of sleep," Keza countered.

"Stop arguing," Horace interrupted, eir voice muffled by the mask. "I'm going either way."

Horace stood back up, then jumped into the

bay, trying eir best not to rock the boat. E still caught Keza's surprised cry before the water dulled all outside sounds, and when e resurfaced, she was low in the boat, claws digging into its side.

"Remember, no pulling at the mask!" Rumi warned.

"May the stars guide you, even all the way down there," Keza added.

Horace waved at them, then turned to swim towards the six lights under a fast-darkening sky. Despite the protection of the two cliff-like arms wrapping around the bay, the high winds drove the water into powerful crests, and Horace struggled to move through them. Once closer to the lights and, e hoped, the Sea Spirit's mystery, e dove down.

The constant pattering of rain faded out, dulled by the water around em. E had always been a good swimmer, carried by the strength of eir muscles, and all the training with Keza served em well when the occasional current pulled at em, trying to swerve Horace from eir path.

Ahead, the six large lights shone, beacons near the sea floor. In the ambient darkness, the lights of the Sea Spirit were almost blinding, the only point of interest in the surrounding haze.

Then lightning flashed, and the bottom of the bay lit up, stunning em into immobility.

A gigantic structure emerged from the sea floor like fingers from a hand, but snapped and broken in parts, the angles wrong. Coral coated large swaths of it, clinging to the frame in unequal and jutting patterns that gave the whole a crooked and haunted look. The overall shape resembled a sphere elongated at the end, like it'd been pinched and stretched, and the structure itself reminded Horace of the metal bands holding barrels, if half of it laid on the rocky bottom. The Sea Spirit's lights were attached to this monstrosity, and under them lay a chaos of coral-covered plaques, rotten wood, and a miscellany of debris e couldn't identify.

The vision faded as quickly as it'd emerged, the lightning gone, and Horace hurried onward. This had been the signal for the Storm Catcher to begin whatever this ritual was. Aliyah was coming, and e still had no idea how to help. As e got closer to the structure, eir ears hurt from the dive, and eir lungs started to burn. Horace pulled the lever for air, and it flowed through the mouth piece and into eir lungs, fresh and dizzying. It worked! Reassured and excited, e took in the full breadth of this strange reef.

It stretched across the bottom of the bay, metal-and-coral fingers reaching for the surface, easily a hundred feet tall. E felt minuscule compared to it, an ant next to a giant, and with the six lights' glow behind em, no longer blinding Horace, e had eir first view of the interior. Instead of dark emptiness, e found more coral-covered debris swarming with life, schools of fish sometimes disappearing in a forest of algae farther down. Large panels of rotten wood remained, cloistering off sections, their colours lost to paint an ambient gloom. Horace swam inside, along broken remnants of what might have been a wall, eir mind trying to piece together what it had been.

Then e caught a first glimmer of gold, floating through the algae. E told emself it was the outside lamps, reflecting off something, but a second gold light emerged from behind a thick mound of coral, and a third drifted down. *Fragments*, it had to be. Cold fear seeped into em. How had e not thought of this? But they'd been in Alleaze for over a month, and the only time e'd seen Fragments was at the shrine the Archivist had brought em to, at the edge of town. They'd been far away, and Horace had gotten it into their head that both the city and the Bay were safe.

Aliyah had warned em. They'd known the Sea Spirit was a Fragment, had sensed it, and none of them had really thought that one through. Now e had dived into deep, stormy waters, and a stream of golden light emerged from eir surroundings. E swam backward, only to be cut off by more Fragments. Horace blinked hard, but eir limited vision wasn't deceiving em. Those weren't the big shards e'd grown accustomed to on the surface, but hundreds of tiny ones, floating together in yellow rivers. Despair curled in eir stomach as the Fragments swirled around em, a whirlpool coming ever closer.

E had been a fool to dive down, to think e could help Aliyah, or solve the mystery of the Sea Spirit. The Fragments tightened their spin around em, and e closed eir eyes, unable to bear the golden glow anymore. E would die here, the air in Rumi's device running out while they possessed em, repeating whatever endless motion they had in mind. E only had two wishes: that it'd be painless, and quick, and e'd have no idea what eir body was doing, and that e might serve as a distraction for the Fragments, allowing Aliyah to remain unnoticed longer.

E didn't have much hope for either.

The glare turned so harsh it went through eir eyelids, and as the Fragments made their final approach, Horace couldn't help eir curiosity. E peeked. The blinding light of a hundred golden shards was the last e saw as they clung to eir skins, countless pinpricks of pain, like a thousand tiny shocks.

Ne stands before the grand wooden panelling, nir eyes glued to the majestic creature carved out of it. Scales and feathers in bright teal and purple, two deep red eyes that seem to move with nem, and powerful wings stretching. It is striking, and nir dormant anxiety turns into trepidation.

"You have paid your due," Captain Siritz says. She is so tall, and beautiful in her own way, with her cascade of white hair braided haphazardly and her easy blue eyes. They rest on nem, now, captivating. "Roll your destiny, if you dare."

Of course ne dares. Ne didn't come here for the fancy wheels of fortune or deadly card games. Ne knows the secret of the Sea Spirit, knows its ultimate lottery, and has given everything for this chance. It beckons, now, so ne steps forward and presses the tail. A soft tune fills the air, the melody of a legend, and a single, black stone rolls out into the beast's beak. Ne doesn't need to touch it to know what is inscribed on it—is too stunned to do so, really. The lightning vault. All the riches ne can carry. A new life, soon.

"Congratulations," the Captain says. "Looks like you're coming with us into the next storm. Shouldn't be too long, with all that rain."

The storm is finally raging outside. Ne says finally, but it has only taken three days. Captain Siritz is right: the downpour has been relentless, and it's no surprise to see it turn for the worse. Or better, as far as nir is concerned.

Light flashes through the windows as ne stands in front of the lever. It looks so ordinary, all black, placed into the wall without any special casing or engraving. It could be any lever, if not for the grand doors besides: reinforced and sealed through magic, circular with a crack down the middle, lightning-shaped.

Captain Siritz is waiting. So is ne—for some dramatic words, or a signal ne is allowed to pull the lever, allowed to raise the Lightning Hands, to grasp the sky's power and open the vault with it. All ne gets *is an impatient quirk of the Captain's eyebrows.*

Ne pulls.

Something is wrong with this storm.

She'd been warned about it, but what had Archivist Eller not cautioned her about, really? Just her luck that they'd be right, this one time.

Captain Siritz has flown through hundreds of storms, and she can tell this one's different. How, she's not sure. Whatever it is, though? She blames it for the malfunction. Never, ever have the Lightning Hands refused to raise. And Histories be cursed, she needs them up before the Sea Spirit eats shit.

None of the engineers were much help, either. All sensors normal, as far as they could tell. Their best guess was that the crystal wasn't pushing any magic into them, so they'd have to be drawn out manually. The sort of thing you did from the top, before the storm. Whatever. She's seen worse. The ship has seen worse. They'll get through this.

Fucking Lightning Hands.

Water slides over her coat, desperate to find a way in, to soak her like it drenched her hair. It sticks to her forehead as she kneels by the tallest of the copper rods. Manual lift didn't work. Or rather, it didn't hold. The copper rods rose all right, then they went right back down in a cacophony so loud it briefly buried the thunder. And the storm is intensifying. She'd prefer to have all five, but just the one is enough to open the vault. Just the one is enough to power her ship for another year or two. If only she can get it to stay up.

The wooden base is slick under her fingers. Water fills the runes etched into it, the original legend of the Sea Spirit and its defiance of lightning. They should be shining bright and blue in this storm, but their light is dimmed. Captain Siritz has left the art of carving and telling to others, but this is her ship and her story. She pulls her long knife out, and starts deepening the lines, one strike at a time.

The Sea Spirit never fell to lightning. Her Sea

Spirit can't either. She needs the world to listen to this story, to hold the Hands up.

She is still carving, minutes or hours later, when the lightning hits.

Water. Water all around em—her? No, em. E was deep in water, and eir fingers burned. E had them buried in coral, was pulling at it as if to break off parts, and a hundred tiny cuts had appeared on eir fingers. Eir lungs burned, too. Horace grasped at eir face in a panic. E still had the mask, Rumi's mask, the breather. Horace pulled the lever, and air flowed in. E wasn't drowning, not yet.

What—

E'd been down there, in the remnants of an ovoid structure. There had been Fragments. They had dived on em, into em … hadn't they? It was hard, to pull through the confusion of images, the shifting sense of self—especially here, eir body floating, the numbness of cold water in stark contrast to the flaring pain of small cuts all over em. E felt sick, and weak, and lost.

Your pain is my pain.

Aliyah's distorted voice, full of power and life, struck through em. E hadn't heard it so much as felt it, but e spun about in search of it.

Horace was at the top of the structure—the *ship*, eir mind provided, with a certitude e didn't understand—near a rotten out piece of wood now overgrown with coral, which e'd been trying to break through. E couldn't fathom why, but the urge still pounded within em.

Aliyah floated above eir head, surrounded by a swirl of golden particles, their own eyes shining in pale green light. They had transformed, but algae now sprung from their arms where Horace had gotten used to twigs and leaves, and instead of the usual thick taproots for legs, Aliyah had grown hundreds of smaller, fragile-looking fine roots. Fragments clung to them, tiny specks of gold, a beautiful and deadly cloud.

Your joy is my joy.

Horace stared, as entranced now as e had been the first time, in Trenaze's Grand Market. A stream of gold rushed out of the ship below, and for a brief moment it created a head, feathers, a long body with fins and wings, curling in the water. Memories of teal and purple flashed through eir mind, and Horace fought a bout of dizziness, the watery world spinning around em. E had seen these things.

Your life is my life.

The form of the Sea Spirit vanished, morphing back into a cloud. Aliyah raised their arms, beckoning invitingly.

Your story is my story.

Horace knew what would follow: they'd absorb all these Fragments, and they'd collapse. Here, in the middle of the water. What if they could only breathe through their tree form? E swam up, towards the cloud of Fragments, heedless of what had happened to em last time. Aliyah was there; Fragments only ever cared for them. They'd protect Horace, and Horace would protect them in return.

But the Fragments didn't vaporize; their thin shards didn't turn into thinner mist, as expected. They stopped swirling, floating for an ominous second, and all dove towards Aliyah, sinking into them. Their body arched and stretched and popped, the echo dulled by the water, and terror crashed through Horace. Then a hundred branches sprouted with an audible crack, spreading in the water, flying past Horace and to the coral e'd dug at bare-handed.

They tore through, ripping it apart until they'd cleared the rotten wooden base, then snuck down its holes. Horace stayed frozen, surrounded by dozens of roots and branches as they crawled into the structure, wrapping around it, then … pulled? A mechanical clank echoed, and slowly the roots emerged, dragging with them a metallic helix. It went up and up and up, until it pierced the water's surface, and still it rose, far beyond Horace's sight. E only knew it stopped by the temporary immobility of the roots.

Without the Fragments' golden glow, the roots were a darker shape in dark waters. Horace waited, eir heart pounding, expecting them to vanish, resorbing into Aliyah. When they didn't, panic rose within em in a steady wave. Horace swam along the roots, towards eir friend's body. Something *different* was happening, and e didn't know what to do about it, how to help. Maybe if e was closer … maybe they'd communicate something? It was a desperate idea, with nothing to back it. Aliyah had never grown such a monstrous number of branches or roots. As best as e could tell, they clung to the metallic structure, holding it up. Where had they found the energy? Had the Fragments—

E reached Aliyah themself, and their thinness stunned em into stillness. They had almost nothing left, only the frailest of trunks, and the sharp bark of their cheek felt hollow and brittle. Horace mouthed their name, reached for them, terrified they'd never survive a return to their elven shape.

Lightning struck.

The branches near Horace clamped down on em, yanking em tight against Aliyah, pressing the breathing mask against their chest and cocooning the both of them. Even through the wood, e glimpsed the flash of light, felt power through the water. Had it hit the metal rod? Coursed down? A multitude of small cracking pops echoed, thrumming in eir ears, and the pressure on em released.

E was free, and so was Aliyah—free from the branches, a drenched elf thinned to the bones, their lips parted and their expression a mix of exhaustion and pain.

Below, a seventh light had turned on.

They had caught a storm.

8

Setting Sail

To Horace's great relief, Rumi and Keza had been the first thing e'd seen upon breaking the surface. They'd known the meaning of the swirling golden light below, or that the branches emerging from water could only signify Aliyah had transformed, and known how often it resulted in them collapsing. So they'd brought the boat about, and a lucky lightning strike had shone enough light for them to reunite.

By the time the first Alleazan ships had returned to the docks, the group was already hidden in the Wagon, drenched. Keza had carried Aliyah back; once Horace had been certain they still breathed, e'd found all of eir strength had left em and crumbled in the small boat. It had taken everything to trudge back home on eir own two feet, and e couldn't remember ever feeling so exhausted in eir life.

"You sure had quite the swim, huh?" Rumi had commented, but e didn't think it had anything to do with the physical exertion.

The Fragments had possessed em, they must have, for em to exit the ship and swim to the coral above, scraping at it with all eir might. Eir body felt miles away, difficult to inhabit, as if they hadn't deserted it entirely. E wondered why they had at all.

Horace tried to sleep it off, and had no trouble doing so, with how tired the ordeal had left em. The sun was well past noon when e woke up. Someone had bandaged all the cuts on eir fingers, although not in time to stop em from leaving a few stains. E dragged emself out of bed, belatedly realizing Aliyah hadn't been in it when e found them tucked in on the two-seater. Still out, still far thinner than they'd been when they'd arrived in Alleaze.

They'd need to eat when they'd wake up. Chances were it wouldn't be today, but e probably should get something in em, too. Horace's only sign of hunger was a dull ache, but when had a good meal not helped em feel better? E sliced an array of mushrooms Keza had foraged from the woods, slapped them in a pan with way too much butter, and scarfed them down once cooked. It didn't do much for eir mood, and e was still staring at eir empty plate in confusion when Rumi and Keza hopped inside, in the middle of what sounded comfortingly like bickering.

"I don't care about the ride, shortscales. They show up here to mess with us, and I'm kicking their asses back into their pretty little—Horace!"

E waved at Keza, then gestured at eir empty plate. "Hi. Sorry, didn't leave any."

"Never mind that. You missed training."

"Oh." It *was* past noon. Heat rushed to eir cheek, eir throat tightening. E hadn't meant to skip!

"She's messing with you," Rumi said. "Can't

be nice to people and let them know you're happy to see them up and all that."

"I'm happy to see you both!" e declared.

Keza huffed at them, and climbed part of the ladder. "Yeah, sure, *whatever*. I'll be keeping watch for angry cityfolk."

She scurried up onto the roof, and Horace turned to Rumi. E didn't need to voice the question.

"Don't know if you noticed them celebrating through the storm, but when the thunder left and the rain cleared, they all saw the big metal pole held by roots in the middle of the Bay, and the cheering and drinking stopped. Silence since, but I think that's about as normal as the Storm Catcher surviving, and I'm sure our good friend will pay a visit sooner rather than later."

Rumi was right. Adelar showed up with the setting sun, this time flanked by two of the four original guards. They must have decided the Wagon's inhabitants had no intention of running away since they hadn't already.

Keza leaped down from the platform to meet them, leaving Rumi and Horace to watch from above. Between her staff, her raised fur, and her battle-ready posture, she didn't need any words to set them all on edge. Adelar raised his hands, palms out.

"Please. We need to speak with the Storm Catcher."

"They're resting," Horace said. "It could be days before they're up and about, let alone in any state to talk."

"But … what they did … we've never witnessed anything like it."

"I don't see what the big problem is," Rumi piped up. "Aliyah did what you asked for. Your storm got caught, and you got your seventh light. Just get on with your business as usual, negotiate your positions and all that. Surely the Sea Spirit wouldn't want you to *ignore* the seventh light!"

Adelar clopped unhappily at the rebuttal. "Please send word when Master Aliyah awakens. No Storm Catcher has ever returned. Alleaze would hear what they have to say."

They would have to wait, the same as Horace,

Rumi, and Keza—and the wait proved excruciating. Horace had never been patient to begin with, but this felt worse in a hundred different ways. E was tired, so tired, unable to focus even on games of saira. Yet after the first night, sleep became difficult. Whenever e closed eir eyes, e saw an enormous ovoid ship, the carving of a great teal and purple creature circling its bulk. E felt water battering eir skin, a storm pounding on em, lightning in the distance—then not. The dreams were vivid enough to wake em, and e'd lay there, restless and alone in eir bed, thinking of Aliyah's nightmares and the countless stories they'd told, of a world with flying ships and magical crystals.

It took four days for Aliyah to wake, and by then, Horace's memories had begun to fade and eir energy returned. E welcomed Aliyah with fresh seafood sautéd in garlic and a gigantic cookie e'd baked in the pan, in a single block. They ate, and laughed, and for an hour all four of them pretended all was normal, as if the Wagon was rolling its way towards their next destination, and not immobilized in a city confused by the unexpected turn of their very holy ritual. Once dinner was over, however, Aliyah set their cutlery down.

"Tell me what is happening out there. I do not remember everything, but I—The Sea Spirit is no more."

Knots reappeared in Horace's stomach. "So it was really all those Fragments?"

They inclined their head in a nod. "I believe they lured someone to raise a … lightning rod of sorts. Horace, you were… You should not have come."

"I'm fine." E'd done eir best to *sound* fine, but the strangled hurt in eir own voice surprised em. *You should not have come.* It stung, an unexpected rejection, and the compounded failures of eir life reared its ugly head, whispering that this was a prelude to the end. E pushed the feeling away. "I know it's dangerous, Aliyah. I don't care. I want to be there. As long as I'm there with you, I trust you to keep me safe, and I—I want you to trust I can catch you."

Aliyah studied em, and for once their silence was almost unbearable. They clung to their mug tighter. "All right. I apologize. You—all of you, in truth—you are my team. It may be difficult, but I must accept that you chose this, even if I did not."

"You make it sound like you carry the whole world," Keza remarked. "Take it easy. People gotta handle themselves."

Horace pressed eir lips very tight. The Archivists thought Aliyah *did* carry the whole world, if their Hero talk was anything to go by. It weighed so heavily on them, though, and sharing the Archivists' belief would only add to the burden.

"Perhaps," they said to Keza, sounding unconvinced. "Regardless, the Fragments are no longer here, but I do not know what this means for Alleaze's life cycle."

"Might wanna try to think of something," Rumi said. "Adelar was here the day after, and mighty flustered about it."

"Why do we even care?" Keza's question had

come out almost a growl. "It's their problem. Let them figure out what it means."

"No." Aliyah wrapped their hands around an empty mug and closed their eyes. "I knew, when the Sea Spirit chose me, that it was a Fragment. I knew what happened when I approached them. I … believe I am supposed to, or that it is a good thing, but that does not lessen my responsibility here. I may not have all the answers, but I will think of something to say. I want…" They stopped, opened their eyes, then looked at each of them in turn. "I want to leave places better than we find them, not worse."

Horace loved that idea. To not only travel but help wherever they went. E grinned at Aliyah and wrapped eir large hands around theirs. "We can totally do that!"

That night, Horace got the best sleep e'd had since receiving the Sea Spirit's guidance. It felt right, to have Aliyah tucked into eir arms, the cold wall at eir back as they shared the narrow mattress. No memories haunted em, and although Aliyah did wake from nightmares, as they so often did, they squeezed eir hand with a relieved sigh and returned to sleep. Horace held them tighter. E had missed it, too.

The following day, they sent an invitation to Adelar to come drink tea with the Storm Catcher. He showed up less than an hour later, in full rainbow regalia, and he'd lost the last two guards. Horace prepared pepperoot tea and a plate of dry biscuits to dip into the tea. Adelar startled at the larger interior when he stepped inside the Wagon, but his gaze locked onto Aliyah without a single comment about the abnormal amount of space. He bowed deeply.

"Storm Catcher. I came to hear what the Sea Spirit had to say."

Aliyah sat on the other side of the table, hands around their tea cup, a mask of calm hiding their tension. They had been even quieter than usual this morning.

"I know why it chose me," they said. "It needed change, and for change, it needed someone unbound by your traditions. There will be no more Storm Catchers."

Their words carried a strange gravitas, and Horace found e couldn't tear eir gaze away from them. It reminded em of the captivating impact of their tree chant—of *your story is my story*—but softer, more natural.

"The cycles are over. No longer will the Sea Spirit call for help when its powers dwindle, as it will replenish itself with every storm. Your Storm Catcher lives in the Bay permanently, and it is Alleaze's responsibility to ensure it never sinks again."

"What … what about the Festival? The Guidance?"

"You may still receive guidance, and I believe your current means remain the best way to do so. When, and under what circumstances it is now acceptable to do so, however, is up to you. Whether you wait for inclement weather or a fixed period of time, the Sea Spirit clearly trusts in your judgment. It has faith in you—as do I. But we must be on our way. I trust Alleaze will respect its bargain?"

Adelar bowed deeper. "We will, Storm

Catcher. And I hope the Sea Spirit's faith in us is warranted."

He never touched his pepperoot tea, instead backing out of the door, to vanish into the city. Horace had no idea whether he had been convinced, unhappy, or excited. Adelar Hilstorm was as good as Aliyah at hiding the emotions roiling inside.

"Why not tell them?" e asked when the door closed behind Adelar. "Don't they deserve to know their Sea Spirit was a bunch of Fragments?"

"Does it matter?" Aliyah asked in turn. "The Fragments called to *me* this time, and in doing so they changed the nature of this ritual. Alleaze has told itself a story for decades—centuries, perhaps—and it has shaped who they are. Who am I, to declare it a lie? What does it help? I would rather guide them through the upheavals of my actions with the tale they know. Perhaps, in time, they will change its nature on their own."

Two days later, they received confirmation

that Jameela had been granted the captaincy of the *Pegasus* and would be preparing for departure. The time had come to negotiate the details of their passage.

"When you indicated four people, so many days ago, you didn't say you wanted to bring the giant Wagon," Jameela said, her tone flat save for an inkling of bemusement. "One would think that'd be an important point of contention, on a ship headed for a long haul across the ocean, where space's tight and weight matters."

They had rolled into the docks under a light drizzle, the Wagon causing its share of whispers as it snaked through the busy crowd, wheels creaking. By the time they stopped near the *Pegasus*, Jameela had strolled down the gangplank to stand in front of it, hands on their hips.

Rumi had ridden on the top platform and climbed down at a leisurely pace Horace thought bordered on offensive. When he reached the ground, he stretched, and the salesman persona sank into him, softening the anxious lizard into a confident interlocutor. "You didn't seem interested in the details."

"That is *not* a detail. Takes a lot of room."

Rumi waggled his finger with a victorious clack of teeth. "It *provides* room. There's more space inside than it occupies, for a start, and all four of us sleep in there instead of taking up your bunks." He walked around Captain Jameela as he talked, his slow circle eventually bringing him back the Wagon, to which he offered an affectionate pat. "What's more, we have a cold box in there and could carry delicacies your crew never gets so far out in the ocean. And the Wagon has my workshop, with which I can turn the *Pegasus* into one of the most clever and comfortable ships to ever set sail. You wouldn't believe the things one can do with a few scrap materials and a very fast brain."

He tapped the side of his head, and Jameela huffed.

"Had that sales pitch in you since you first

showed up, eh?" She waved away Rumi's upcoming answer and kept going. "You'll have plenty of time to convince me I didn't get the raw end of a deal on the way, but it's still heavy. I'll have to rethink what supplies we're bringing, so I want you around tomorrow to discuss the *details*, as you put it. Regardless, a promise's been made, and you kept your end and then some."

"Can do," Rumi said, and that seemed good enough for Jameela, who was eager to move on.

"Should've seen everybody's face when they learned the Storm Catcher's conditions. Choosing their captain? I didn't even need to trade tokens in negotiations! Between that and all the extras I get to keep for this cycle—one which is bound to be rockier than most—I bet I made quite a few enemies. But that's a problem for Future Jameela, as we say."

"Don't know who's we, but it's not me," Rumi countered with an anxious twist of his tail. Horace held back a snicker. Rumi would *never* be this calm about future problems, no.

"Regardless," Jameela said, "We'll clear some space for your Wagon, if you can get it across the gangplank."

Rumi's skittering laughter was music to Horace's ears.

"That's the easiest part of all, my good captain," he said. "You'll see soon enough."

Jameela rolled her eyes, but when they returned several days later to finally board, she remained conveniently in sight of the Wagon, even as she ordered sailors about. She never quite stopped watching Rumi, and Horace caught the widening of her eyes as his friend ran scaled hands over the wheels, bringing teal glyphs to life all around the inside. The wheels split, one half transforming into a large, rounded foot while the rest unfurled a mechanical machine akin to a leg. The Wagon stretched up, jerking forward and back as it rose, then walked right over the gap between docks and deck.

Wood creaked plaintively as it stepped onto the *Pegasus*, and for a moment Horace worried the deck would give way under them—that they'd crash through it and the hull and into the water, putting Keza's swimming lessons to an early test—but it quieted again as the Wagon refolded its legs. Two prongs stayed out, stabilizing it so it wouldn't roll in either direction.

"I'll stake it down once you're certain of the location," Rumi told Jameela. "Shouldn't slide around even in the worst storms."

That earned him a snort. "We'll see about that when we hit them." Jameela clapped Rumi's back then turned back towards the crew. "All right, sailors new and old, gather round."

Every sailor on deck stopped or finished up their tasks and moved to Captain Jameela, forming a loose circle. From the top of the Wagon, Horace had an incredible view of it and eir eyes remained glued to the group even as e nudged Aliyah to make sure they watched, too. The sailors each extended an arm out, holding a stone much like the one Keza had drawn from the Sea Spirit's guidance—sailor stones.

"Today we leave on our first voyage. We salute the Sea Spirit for its guidance and trust, and as we sail out, we pray it stays with us. May our stones be beacons, and may its love never fail us."

One by one, they placed the stones in a net by the *Pegasus'* mast, placed their palm on the wood, then returned to their previous occupation. Horace was so fascinated by it, e barely registered the snap of sails catching in the wind, and the moment the ship moved away. All of a sudden, Alleaze's square buildings were receding in the distance, faster than e'd have expected. E gripped the Wagon's railing, sad e'd been asked not to go on the deck while they set sail. E wanted eir feet on it, to fully experience the moment, but there would be time, wouldn't there? There would be lots of time.

They passed by the Storm Catcher, its partially rusted metal shining in the sunlight, dark roots still clinging to it. Horace had spent eir last days in Alleaze mulling over Aliyah's words and their decision to retain the truth.

Stories have power, Archivist Kol had told em, and in that they both seemed to agree. Perhaps he'd been right. Maybe, just like Alleaze needed to be spared the truth to thrive in the future, Aliyah would be better off without the burden of being the Hero.

A shadow fell over the ship, drawing Horace out of eir thoughts—one of the cliffs that formed the Bay's arms, enclosing it. The sheer rock face rose above, and then it passed too, as quickly as it had appeared.

And beyond it, the blue. Blue as far as eir eyes reached, sparkling in the sun, barred by the occasional dancing line of sea foam. It lost itself in the distance, growing hazy until it merged with the pale grey of the sky. They sailed into it, the winged horse at the ship's prow breaking the waves at a slight angle. Horace couldn't help emself any longer: e ran down the ladder, out of the Wagon, and to the front, clinging to the railing and leaning forward. The wind caught in eir curls, and e grinned.

There was no end to the blue; no end to the

world, to its promises—to its mysteries. Horace might not fully understand what had happened below the waves, or what the vivid scenes e'd lived meant, but e didn't mind the mystery. All e wanted to be there for Aliyah when they needed, and to experience the world with eir friends.

THE STORY CONTINUES....

Fate and friendship brought Horace, Rumi, Keza, and Aliyah together in Rumi's sentient self-propelling wagon. They seek the forest haunting Aliyah's dream, hoping for answers about the elf's past and unique abilities.

When they undertake the ocean crossing, they don't expect the sailors' fearsome myths to come to life. At sea, the Fragments that roam the world have coalesced into a gigantic beast — the kraken of legends. The crew may have bested countless storms, but no amount of sea-worthiness can save the ship from the wrath of its colossal tentacles. If they want to escape, the wagon's team will need to unravel more of the Fragments' mysteries, and learn to listen beyond the murmur of the sea.

On the third morning, eir sanitary pit dig finished, Horace joined the group building new shelters, using trimmed branches and the trees' gigantic leaves. Some of them sprawled longer than Horace's arms, glistening and green, vegetation the likes of which e'd never seen in the desert. E'd been impressed by the tall forest on Alleaze's side of the Tesrima Ridge, but although those stretched upward to the sky, their trunks so large e couldn't surround em with eir arms, their leaves had been small rows of spiky points common to evergreens. It would never cease to fascinate Horace, how varied plant life was across the world, from the thick and barbed leaves of succulents in the deserts, to the endlessly vertical trees outside Alleaze, and now these wonderful specimens. Horace spent as much time waving the long leaves around, making *woosh* sounds, as e did placing them atop their makeshift constructions to build roofs.

Once, eir wide swoops clipped Millicent and the older sailor stumbled, more out of surprise at the large green thing in her face than any real strength in the blow. Unfortunately for Horace, several crew members saw it and surrounded em with fake outrage, each with their own "weapon", ready to avenge her. Horace tanked the first two leaf slaps, too confused to dodge, but before long eir reflexes kicked in, and e brought eir own leaf up as a shield, parrying with it. The sailors cackled and redoubled their efforts, so Horace put everything e had into the spontaneous make-believe fight, grinning ear to ear.

They were still doing this strange dance when Keza discovered them.

"Training without me?" she asked. "I'm wounded."

E turned toward her voice only to find an odd amber sphere flying at eir face. It, too, caught em off guard, and it smacked into eir nose. Tears blurred eir vision from the sudden pain, but through them e thought e saw the ball hit the ground and *bounce*. Keza caught it up again and grinned.

Order the next book now at

books2read.com/storiesfromthedeep-nerezia

Join the Newsletter to get all extras and never miss an update

About the Author

Claudie Arseneault is an easily-enthused aromantic and asexual writer with a never-ending cycle of obsessions but an enduring love for all things cephalopod and fantasy (together or not!). She writes stories that centre platonic relationships and loves large casts and single-city settings, the most notable of which are the City of Spires series (2017-2023) and Baker Thief (2018).

In addition to her own fiction, Claudie has co-edited Common Bonds (2021), an anthology of aromantic speculative short stories. She is a founding member of The Kraken Collective, an alliance of self-publishing SFF authors, and the creator of the Aromantic and Asexual Characters Database.

Find out more at claudiearseneault.com

Start another book
from the Kraken Collective!

Craving more fun bite-sized queer fantasy? Party of Fools is a comedic adventure with big Final Fantasy vibes where two rebels tag along as the Chosen One and imperial Hero escapes scrutiny to go on a worldwide food tour—that is, if she can escape the Capital.

Dig into another novella lead by a non-binary protagonist and thaes close-knit group of friends with *The Shimmering Prayer of Sûkiurâq*, A deliciously queer magical person story in a secondary world with floating cities and airships, perfect for fans of She-Ra and Steven Universe.

Find these books and more at
www.krakencollectivebooks.com

Acknowledgements

Here we are, at the end of the first third of these novellas, and the last of them that was offered on Kickstarter. So first, a final thank you to all of you who supported this project almost a year ago now. Without that initial impetus, I would not have been justified in keeping this regular a schedule with them, and would have needed to turn to other, perhaps more profitable projects. But you all believed in my weird little novellas promising fun board games and a mix of high stakes, epic moments and the quiet hours that friends spend with one another. You believed in stories that shove romance completely at the backstage, both for the characters and the world. You believed in a format that was more bite-sized and episodic than is traditional. By now I've run out of Kickstarter money, and must hope that the series continues to fund itself, that others will believe in these things as strongly as I do. Regardless of the outcome, thank you for getting me this far!

Behind this book is an entire team of talented people: my cover artist, Eva, who continues to bring to life my universe in one long canvas; my line artist, Vanessa, whose designs for the crew always bring me great joy, and my super editor, Lynn, who ensures the actual text is clean and crisp. Special thanks, also, to Cedar and Quartzen and Lynn (again!), who through reading and brainstorming continue to help bring these stories to bright, vibrant life.

In addition to them, I have an incredible support network, both in real life and online. Huge thank you to my friends who are first in line to get their copies, to my fellow Kraken Collective authors (and many others authors around the internet) with whom I share the self-publishing struggles and can commiserate, to every reader and blogger out there who buys, features, reviews, comments, or even just secretly reads.

To my partner and my family, who follow me down this road. There is a lot of love to go around, and I am so thankful for all of it.